I0664371

SWEDE AMONG THE REDNECKS

The Language That Just Won't Stay Buried

ESSAYS WRITTEN FOR *NORDSTJERNAN*
BY ULF KIRCHDORFER

NORDSTJERNAN
FÖRLAG, NEW YORK

For my Mother

Swede Among the Rednecks: The Language That Just Won't Stay Buried
Essays written for Nordstjernan

Nordstjernan Förlag, New York 2015
www.nordstjernan.com
1.800.827.9333

Swede Among the Rednecks
©Copyright 2015 Ulf Kirchdorfer / Nordstjernan Förlag
Design: Dan Arbello
Cover photo: Anne Clark/iStock photo
Fonts: Edita by TypeTogether, Bemio by Joe Prince/Lost Type, Lisboa by Fountain

ISBN: 978-0-9968460-1-1
First English edition. Printed in the USA.
Nordstjernan Förlag
Swedish News, Inc.
Book Services
P.O. Box 1710
New Canaan, CT 06840

Contents

1 . . . . Swede Among the Rednecks

5 . . . . Table Culture

7 . . . . Fathers and Sons

9 . . . . Chucky vs. the Dala Horse

13 . . . . Arrivingor Not

17 . . . . Televinken Forever

19 . . . . The Spirit Of the Games

23 . . . . The "Sinful" Ingmar Bergman

27 . . . . "Keep Cool but Care"

29 . . . . Glögg and Julskinka. Okay, but Stjärngosse?

33 . . . . Musings on, of and by a "Certified Swede"

37 . . . . "My Lawn is My Castle"

41 . . . . Oh, the Story I Found!

45 . . . . My Swedish Crime Drama

49 . . . . NOT Certifiably Swedish!

53 . . . . Broadening Horizons

57 . . . . On Eggshells

61 . . . . A Swede Appreciates Fourth of July

63 . . . . Where Swedes Fear to Tread

67 . . . . Commendable Sweden!

69 . . . . Pippi Longstocking Censored, Swedes Next

73 . . . . My Waterloo with ABBA

77 . . . . Finding the Middle Way

81 . . . . Looking for a Church

85 . . . . Distressed Furniture

89 . . . . Lund: Of Pocket Knives and Flashlights

93 . . . . Showers in Freedom

97 . . . . Print of Peace

99 . . . . Stubborn and så "jävla envisa"

101 . . . . Of Mom and Monkeys

105 . . . . IKEA and the Great Chocolate Heist

109 . . . . Welcome to Sweden

113 . . . . The Dangerous Kitchen

117 . . . . From My Mobile Office

119 . . . . Good vs. Evil Was Once Clear. Or Was It?

123 . . . . Summer Dream

127 . . . . The Language That Just Won't Stay Buried

131 . . . . Why I Love Torturing my Students with William Faulkner

137 . . . . My Beef with 50+ Commercials

141 . . . . A Brief History of the American Family Vacation

145 . . . . The Great American Lawn Mowing

147 . . . . Summer School in the Garden

Swede Among the Rednecks

I am writing this against the backdrop of cotton fields, peanut silos, and full knowledge that even in the city I live in I am surrounded by rednecks. Of course rednecks are stereotypes just as they are real people. And is it not so also with Swedes?

What is it that makes me Swedish? I have wondered and continue to contemplate where I live in the south. What is a redneck for that matter? A guy wearing a baseball cap, driving a pickup truck, and hanging a Confederate flag in front of his house or trailer? Perhaps.

What is a Swede? A *sill*-eating Social Democrat commuting to work by pedaling in *trätofflor* on a bicycle? Perhaps.

In my case, I can see the black passport with crowns that I had to turn in when I became a U.S. citizen in my mid-20s. I also know that I have a stack of Pelle Svanslös books, horizontal, on my bookshelf. It would be too much to say that the Svanslös is symbolic of having severed my ties with Sweden or the ability to find out what it means to be Swedish. But it is not easy to reach a conclusion about what it means to be Swedish, even what it means to me.

I wish there were some truly scientific, psychological, sociological – keep on adding the qualifying adjectives – test, a kind of shower I could step into and come out of with clean and clear answers, and be given a card with a seal of approval – the way items of food are labeled by those who are chosen to be suppliers to the King of Sweden. There would be a little booklet attached to this card and it would detail what makes me Swedish or a Swede.

In absence of such, I will try not to let my imagination wander too far as I explore the subject. I sense, too, a reluctance to provide a clear and definitive answer. Does this quality make me Swedish? I have not been back to Sweden in so many years, I do not know what a jury of Swedes-in-Sweden would tell me.

I know I am a fairly nice guy and I don't believe in using violence to solve things. That does not mean I can't get angry – I can on occasion – but I think my violent tendencies, if I have to conjure some, come more in the form of stubbornness. To explain, redneck Americans would be more apt to stand on their lawn with a gun and tell someone to get off their land than I would, and they would have more of a John Wayne attitude of getting this kind of work done and letting it be done with, over with, fairly quickly. As a Swede, I would find the whole matter to be festering, lingering with a need to discuss a solution. I cannot imagine a Swedish John Wayne. If there was one, he would be a comedic hit in Sweden.

Recently I brought to work a ceramic Viking and a glass rune stone. I felt a little uneasy about putting them on display. There is something disagreeable and suspicious, at least to me, about people who loudly proclaim their heritage, or focus solely or build their entire existence around one mascot, emblem or team. For example, I know plenty of redneck Americans whose entire lives revolve around the college or professional football team that will have a game once a week. Family, work, even the southern worship of God that is a such a biggie, takes a distant place compared to the Atlanta Falcons, UGA and their bulldog who has an air-conditioned doghouse, or the baseball team of the Atlanta Braves. This is not to say that as a Swede I am immune to appreciating sports or being a fan. I remember watching Ulf Sterner play ice hockey in his "fading" years and my father was quite passionate about ice hockey. But I don't remember masses of Swedes (is there such a thing?) living only for ice hockey. So perhaps my reluctance to proclaim something loudly is Swedish.

I like bland foods, or rather I do not relish what is so popular among redneck southerners, food so spicy as to make you sweat and your stomach to suffer no matter how much over-the-counter medicine is taken after inhaling nachos with hot peppers, or what passes for Mexican food here in the south. In contrast, does my love for *fiskbullar* covered by white sauce make me Swedish?

If I add up some of the external factors or objects I have thus far assembled in my quest to find out what internally makes me Swedish, I have an odd assortment of Pelle Svanslös books, a stubbornness not to be confused with violence, a healthy like of sports, and an aversion to a diet that causes intestinal and other discomfort. And I have a few items I now display at work that are cultural touchstones. Not that it is a competition (but of course it is!), the redneck American does not fare as favorably with a Confederate flag flying history as if it were the present in front of his trailer, gut-wrenching dietary habits, and a John Wayne "get off my lawn or I'll have to shoot you" attitude, followed by, "Hurry up, I am going to miss my football game."

So as I sit eating my open-faced cheese sandwiches with a glass of milk, home for lunch from work, the silence that allows thinking hovering around the kitchen table, I draw the conclusion that I am in my definition of what it means to be Swedish for the long haul, like a Viking traveling and being kind to his family and having an appreciation for beauty, a culture hidden as it is displayed, displayed as it is hidden, a seeker, someone who does not wear his flag on his sleeve.

I have blond hair and I am tall. That does not make me Swedish, yet it does. ❦

Table Culture

The way we use utensils is one indication of our origin.

I remember hearing that during World War II spies gave themselves away by such simple actions as maneuvering utensils during meals. Fascinating stuff in a spy movie that whitewashes the blood of war – who wants to be put to death for using a knife the "wrong" way – but also a lesson in how culture and upbringing stay with us and emerge, no matter how hard we try to assimilate or act like camouflage in our new-found environment.

As a child I got to visit America several times before we finally moved here. I recall using a knife to cut meat into pieces, not bite by bite, but in anticipation of that prolonged period when the beef would be in my mouth after it was slapped on my plate. And there I was cutting one piece, putting it into my mouth, and certainly not returning the knife to its position at 12 o'clock atop my plate.

For years, even when I had my U.S. citizenship, I ate peas by shoving them on top of the outside of my fork, fork curved like a convex bridge across a brook. The cultural divide remained at the dinner table. I found eating peas this way to be natural and the only way. Fellow American diners probably felt as if they were at a dinner theatre while eating with me. But then I had to watch them cut meat into little pieces for themselves as if they were preparing a meal for a child.

Oh, and the things they eat! I am sure it was more true a few decades ago than today, but as a Swede I did not know why Americans had such a craving for "Mexican" food, which they liked hot and spicy, even using the adverbs interchangeably with the compound noun. But having come from the land of boiled potatoes and *fiskbullar* in white sauce, "Ay, caramba!" or "Ay Chihuahua!" didn't pass my lips, though "*fy fan*" – with coughing and downing endless amounts of water with the meal in a useless fire-extinguishing attempt – became part of my M.O. in America.

Of course "Oh, and the things they eat!" was equally easy for Americans to apply to Swedes. Every person I met who found out I was Swedish – no matter their education level or other outward look

– had heard of and asked if I had eaten *lutfisk*. How I hated the way they pronounced it, the "t" transformed into a thud of "d" and an "e" added to boot; how I craved to hear *"Lutfisk!"* and even though I carried a Swedish passport, no, I had not consumed *lutfisk* and was not a lifetime fan.

To this day I remain a stranger in a strange land, I suppose, by making open-faced sandwiches, even atop the flat side of the bagel. I am sure there are Swedes now who sandwich their cheese between two slices of bread, but if that is the case, I hope I never see it.

But there is one double-fisted, beautiful food that to me is uniquely American and which I immediately embraced. The burger. The bigger the better, the burger is a food so wonderful to me not only because of its ravishing taste seduction but probably also because as an immigrant I associated eating the burger with being American.

And back when I first set foot on these shores I was distinctly Swedish in my coffee consumption. It set me apart from Americans, who at the time drank something they called coffee that was light-brown colored water. I remember a particularly horrid taste experience at what was an elegant carwash (a novelty to watch through huge glass windows Cadillacs being soaped, slathered, lathered and bubbled as if they were movie stars of the Golden Era). The coffee was absolutely spit-able, if I may coin such a word. But gradually my taste for strong, dark coffee took hold on America, and now my consumption of it on a daily basis (Sumatra please!) does not make me uniquely Swedish anymore.

Coffee, then, is one food-and-drink related item, something gustatory that has actually succeeded in inhabiting the landscape of the American melting pot. With this observation recorded, it is time to get a cup of coffee, but I think I will have some Marabou milk chocolate with mine. ❦

Fathers and Sons

My father was an absent man and perhaps that is why his presence appears more often now, once I have opened my memory bank. When my brother and I were growing up, he was gone most of the time, traveling and making a living for his family. But before his travels grew to Gulliver proportions and we started school, my father spent Saturday mornings with us.

For some reason my mother left on Saturday mornings, whether to shop or just have some time for herself, but what mattered was that my brother Björn and I got to climb up on our parents' bed, where my father, not a morning person, spun the most marvelous yarns.

Of course we did not know he was a fiction maker or fabulist. And I don't think later in life, when he was firmly entrenched in remaining honest in a business world that was not, those who came into contact with him knew about this part of his inner life. And by then we, too, had forgotten, the chasm or gulf had closed. Not as if by magic but by the hard life of a business man in sales on the road.

Saturday mornings in Stora Harrie, Sweden, were a wonderful world. We learned of Mats and Olle, two boys who were outside playing and fell asleep atop a small hill that had comfortable grass to lie on. Mats and Olle then were able to observe and understand adventures involving *ekorrhissen*, which for some strange reason was used by the squirrels to travel up to a nest of birds. Into this nest a magpie dropped a silver spoon. Logic was out the window, the animals never brutally interacting, and everything made sense. Then, inevitably, the two boys, Mats and Olle, woke up after yet another adventure.

It never occurred to us, certainly not consciously, that Mats and Olle were us, and we did not yet know that my father was drawing from his vast knowledge of mythology to tailor a story finer than any gift someone could have bought us with money.

What saddens me now is that I do not remember the stories my father told us. But, strangely, I experience a kind of warmth when I write about these mornings my father the storyteller spent with my brother and me. It was also one of the few times we did not feud, I bite him or he chase me with a feather, pick your sibling rivalry antics of the moment.

What saddens me more than not remembering the stories is that my father never wrote these stories down. Perhaps he was too tired when he finally set down his suitcase in hotel room after hotel room. I know that he read a great deal, perhaps he needed someone to tell him a story, and that I understand.

My father would have made such a great storyteller if he could have done so "for a living." Instead he had to march to the drumbeat of a captain of industry, and while I never heard him complain (he never complained about anything), his silence became protracted as the years went by. I wonder if he was telling stories inside of his head.

These are the types of questions one asks when one approaches or reaches middle age; realizes the sacrifices one makes even if one likes going to work. I also realize that the older I get, the fewer choices are available, or the paths narrow, as my father used to tell me when I was a clueless teenager.

I hope the inner storyteller, sculptor, painter, patio bricklayer, gardener, knitter, singer, chef lives in and outside of you, and you take the steps necessary to practice what you love besides work. And if you can, leave something tangible behind of your adventures outside of work for your children, grandchildren, nieces or nephews, friends.

This has been one son celebrating life and eulogizing his father, hoping the spirit of imagination lives in you. 🐦

Chucky vs. the Dala Horse

While it surprises some who do not know me when I tell them I listen to country music, it would surprise them even more if I told them I have been a big fan of the *Chucky* movies. Pity those who think I listen to Sibelius (let the melancholic Finn stand in when no one seems to be able to name Swedish composers) and choose Bergman's *The Seventh Seal* for family movie night. For those not in the know, the object of my movie affection in question is Chucky, a not-so-nice doll (or so they say) who comes alive and utters such wonderful lines as, "Don't [insert verb that rhymes with his name] with the Chuck!"

Cute, red-headed – or at least flaxen-haired (depending on the lighting) – little Chucky made quite an impression on moviegoers' wallets. Not a fan of the horror movie genre, I nevertheless liked the little killer doll doing his thing because I interpreted him as embodying a sendup of what it means to be evil. Chuck would also be a great candidate for Swedish Social Services; I guarantee they could not rehabilitate him.

I have such affection for Chucky that when I once saw a doll made in his likeness in a store, I immediately wanted to make him part of our household; sadly, I knew it would be a no-go, my wife finding my fascination with Televinken and his presence in my closet sufficiently creepy.

Why do I bring up Chucky? Is it because I want to discuss his existence and how it interrelates to the Swedish psyche? Not a bad idea, but I have absolutely no answer to that headache. I am telling you about Chucky because I want to contextualize bringing up what, in my opinion, really is his four-legged relative, the *dalahäst*.

That's right, the *dalahäst*. The icon of Swedish heritage that Swedes, or at the very least the makers of the *dalahäst*, take so seriously and tell of its coming into existence in that special province in Sweden where during long and cold winter nights the equine creatures were carved by men in rural poverty.

Somehow that tradition has continued, and to have a *dalahäst* is a must, even in its adulterated, I mean customized, state that includes an optional corporate logo. The *dalahäst* is alive and well on websites with Swedish flags, assuring us that in this world something is handmade and hand painted, and if the photos are to be believed, the craftsmen are not exploited Chinese children inhaling toxic chemicals and ready to jump suicide fences onto asphalt. No, these "fathers" of *dalahästarna* can look toward the lake where the pine they use to make their horses grows fine and free. They probably even take a *fika* when they choose.

Still, something wicked this way comes when I think about a *dalahäst*, no matter its color or size. Maybe it is the shape of the ears, or the fact that the horse is wooden, that makes me think of betrayal and trickery, and not only because of the Trojan horse mythology. That creature just won't – cannot – look you in the eye, and such a presence does not inspire trust, calm. While there are no teeth visible on these glossy creatures, I see them, as if the *dalahäst* was an inhabitant of Picasso's *Guernica*.

I am not sure if hundreds of years ago the carvers did not plant the seed for witches, goblins and trolls to continue in some form of wooden progeny. When an unsuspecting tourist or resident Swede enters a store to buy one or two of these creatures, they are bringing home bad luck or at least tempting good fortune.

Not to worry, though, if you cannot commit this act by actually stepping inside a store in Sweden. Just Google Scandinavian stores in the U.S. or visit online sites where you can have delivered to your home the evil *dalahäst*.

If you think about it, it is kind of "sexy" to acquire more than a pussycat *dalahäst* for your home. Now you are, or soon can be, the proud owner of something sacrosanct that even a soothsayer in old Greece would shake her head at, having looked at the innards of the strange bird, predicting something eventful.

Finally, should you be the owner of a business that sells *dalahästar* and you find your sales going up after publication of this issue of

Nordstjernan, may I ask that you donate part of your increased revenues to the humane society? This has been your correspondent, riding the *dalahäst*. 🐎

Arriving or Not

One of the most beautiful things about being a child is that you have no way of knowing how you really arrive somewhere. You might be excited by the fact that you will board a train or will get to ride a ferry, but the actual journey as a linear process, one that requires the responsibility of getting there, is not of your domain. Instead, you might be awakened from your play-reality into the unfamiliar territory of the sound effect of a train that so happens to be leaving the station. You might wonder why an elderly gentleman is strangely rubbing the shoulders of a young boy eating an ice cream cone. Depending on who your travel chaperones or guardians are, you will have things explained or not.

But then you arrive wherever it is you have been promised you will go, and a whole new world opens up and you are there to explore and enjoy it, not conscious of time, like an adult who knows he or she has one or two weeks of vacation before it is time to return to a demanding boss or exciting job he or she has had to leave behind in the name of leisure. As a child, you collect impressions around you, in some ways much like a writer or poet, only you do not bear the burden of the adult witness who feels the compulsion to make connections and extensions from what has been encountered. You also simply react to your surroundings, or, more like it, you react in and with your surroundings.

What you have read is an adult's preamble into a childhood paradise I call Höllviken. How I long for those summers when we walked and biked to buy ice cream, the memory of green and well-kept hedges, a comfortable heat, all in the outpost of my aunt and uncle's house which was almost on the beach. When I say almost, I vaguely recall that it was the last or second last house before a few sandy steps across a dune barrier into yet another landscape, the vast sea, Baltic

Sea?, where I have very few memories other than just lulling or existing in some pleasant state. Maybe it was zen before I knew it and before children needed zen?

I recall eating dinner on the beautiful lawn with my aunt and cousins Henrik and Fredrik, and the arrival of my uncle, Bosse, as we called him, a man who always said nice things that immediately were punctuated by, "*va*," and laughter. My aunt, *Moster* Kaje, had married what then was perceived as late in life, but probably was in her early-30s. Her husband sold homes, I did not know the term realtor, and I remember he had a wonderful car that adults reverentially called "Mercedes." He also smoked cigars – and I had never met anyone who smoked cigars. I can still see those cigars, stubby looking ones, a match for my uncle's fingers, his sixth finger if you will.

But such extensions as the one mentioned are made by an adult, and of course any memories I render have been merged with the imagination and coloration of the adult who has developed from a childhood that included such beautiful experiences as summers in Höllviken.

I came back to visit later when I was far across the Baltic Sea and other waters, living in America, a teenager. It was the cold of winter in Höllviken, with a special kind of bright light, and we had yulebord, which culminated in my aunt and me walking with our stretched stomachs on the beach. The gray waters and the wind, the excursion into something memory could not quite connect with what childhood had offered me in Höllviken. Men in oilcloth were out, carrying huge nets with handles, hoops, in which my aunt said they collected amber. I remember one of the men seeing us approach and not wanting to share even a view of the large piece of amber he had collected from the sea.

Such is the emergence of adulthood, the sad reality that sharing of memories will be categorized into positive "only to connect" moments, along with an unwillingness to connect, a disconnection by and from others, voluntary and involuntary. I know that visit on the beach that winter day brought with it a sad beauty, and a beauty that was sad.

There is a difference, and one cannot help but bring in the poet Keats, with his "Beauty is truth, truth beauty." In this Swede's world, beauty and truth, and truth and beauty will reside forever in Höllviken, as I carry it with me like an expatriate his luggage.

My luggage might be on rollers these days, but does that make it any better? This is your correspondent signing off, in a more reflective state this time. ☛

Televinken Forever

He has been with me all these years and throughout, I have heard and continue to hear his voice, "Anita! Anita!" It has a kind of enthusiastic tug-at-your-sleeve insistence, that he will not go away until his curiosity, mixed in with mischief, has been satisfied.

For those who don't know who I am talking about, I state his wonderful name, Televinken. As a child I did not do any etymological investigation of the word; as an adult, I am aware of the clever compounding of the word "television" with a kind of wink and short moment, for those of us who speak Swedish.

While I have since learned that he was to have been a teaching tool, I do not remember Televinken teaching me anything, nor do I remember the programs. I recall only the insistent voice of the little guy, a marionette wearing a cool outfit and having such incredibly large eyes that seemed to go with his personality. And there was the Anita lady, who I might have felt some attraction toward that I could not quite formulate at such an early age.

I know that I had a thin book with a sleeve and an accompanying 45-rpm record featuring Televinken. I do not know what happened to that book. That the book is missing is surprising to me, since I cherished Televinken so and have been able to keep track of other items from childhood, including *Emil i Lönneberga*, *Pelle Svanslös*, *Karlsson på Taket*, *Ture Sventon Privatdetektiv*, and Lego (yes I know it's Danish).

I wanted to have Televinken come live with me, and I vaguely understood from my mother that he was expensive, not in our family budget, or perhaps she did not think that a marionette in his image was a toy that a boy needed.

But my grandmother, ever generous with her purse strings, managed to place Televinken before me on my birthday. I felt a pang of disappointment that Televinken was not wearing the same outfit he sported on TV, and the red threads that connected his limbs to a wooden cross were hard to coordinate for a young boy, but the overall feeling was one of joy. Televinken, a kind of hero like Tintin for my brother, had come to hang out with me.

While it might seem strange to some to be fascinated by a marionette, the fascination appears to be a cross-cultural one, Pinocchio drawing in audiences across the world, and there is no shortage of dummies or programs featuring dummies and their ventriloquists that even adults pay attention to. Of course many feel that these types of puppets (forgive the use of terminology that is not interchangeable amongst true aficionados of marionettes, ventriloquism, puppetry theatre, et al) are creepy.

My wife is one of those who is not a fan, including of Televinken. You see, even after 23 years of marriage, Televinken is still with me, in what is now our (my wife's and my) house. During various moves and in temporary locations Televinken lived in a box, which, I am sorry to say, did not have air holes, and I allowed him to lie slumped over.

But in our current home, where we have lived for 10 years, Televinken has had a good run hanging from a bar inside a closet. This is the closet where I keep my stuff, and I know my wife does not open the closet because she does not want to see the creepy Televinken.

But to me Televinken represents a bond that happened between a marionette and a Swedish boy, one that brings childhood into the present, something that is worth contemplating every now and then. I am also sure there are other Swedish-Americans out there who have kept something from their past. I hope they have. I would like to hear from them. I wonder and worry about people who grow up and consider themselves too mature to have any such connection with their past.

"Anita! Anita!" Televinken is calling, and I must go.

Until next time, I remain your *skribent*. 🐦

The Spirit of the Games

I am comfortably slouching on the sofa, reading a book or checking my email on that small device that I am convinced one day soon will take the place of the human hand, when I hear the celebratory music of NBC announcing that it is time to watch their coverage of the Winter Olympics. That music almost makes me sit up straight, but wait, not so fast, NBC. It is eerie to me the way the fanfare wants me to celebrate the spirit of the Games and be patriotic. It is a hard sell that is cause for alarm, if we think about it.

If by patriotism you mean that I will feel the hair on my neck stand and also experience goose bumps and a kind of pride of accomplishment, that I get. I was in my study working on a William Faulkner article this weekend when my wife called out to me and I managed to make it into the living room in time to hear four Swedish guys out of breath talk about their win, skis still in hand and wearing those delightful Swedish yellow-and-blue winter hats. That was a moment I felt pride without going overboard and also love for the country I was born in.

Quite frankly, I was surprised that NBC would interview four Swedish guys and not just Americans when they win or almost win an event. In fairness to NBC coverage here in America, they are trying to appeal to the patriotism of Americans. But NBC and other media outlets are sending a mixed message that I find bothersome. On one hand we hear all this talk about the spirit of the Games and how it unites people, and the Games is one of those occasions when politics, even war, comes to a halt.

Not so. Broadcasters on "news" shows, be they labeled liberal, conservative, or in-between, are putting on display smiles, the kinds that show *Schadenfreude*. Or sarcasm laces the so-called reporters' voices. I understand that it is great to beat your opponent and that sports must have a winner. I am all for that, as I believe in and relish competition. But taking such open and ill-natured delight in other countries being losers, and I use the term to signify more than someone who loses a sporting event, has not shown we are truly celebrating the spirit of the Games. Yes, I have been alluding to the constant bashing of the Russians.

I will admit that I am not a fan of Putin. I have made fun of him. After all, what bare-chested man on horseback is not an easy target? And being ex-KGB, that's like saying someone is a former Adolf Hitler storm trooper, and can Vladimir the Great really care about athletes he visits in the hospital with the camera right there shining on his reflecting forehead? Well, to be fair, Hitler did pet his German Shepherd. After reading reports in the media – some relayed with glee – I have made comments to my wife that someone in Putingrad is being or has been executed over such foibles as railings or hotel rooms not being painted in time or for building double-occupancy toilets for cheek-to-cheek conversation.

But is it really necessary to take such delight in the failings of the Russians when it does not have to do with actual athletic competition itself? When I was younger and Sweden played the Soviet Union in ice hockey I remember being in a state of excitement that would probably have made my berserker Viking ancestors proud. My father and I wanted those #&*@%^ Soviets to lose. We wanted their blood. On the ice and off the ice. We hated everything they stood for, their communism, their brutality, and on and on. And I dare say other peace-loving Swedes back then hated the Soviets' guts and made an ugly, open display of emotions running amok. A triumph in hockey was a like victory over evil in those days.

Living in America, I did not have love instilled in me for the Soviet Union or Russia either. But I have detected a cooling-off in the bashing of the Russians. Instead, for some years, we had the Japanese to "hate" (there was Pearl Harbor, and then Japanese automobiles were killing American auto manufacturers), but mostly the Chinese are now the ones we fear and "hate," as they own America, are threatening to take over the world, are not listening to the U.S., and violating human rights in a way we are told rivals perhaps only North Korea.

A lot of baggage to saddle onto the Olympic events in Russia this year. And is it not interesting that the Chinese are not being bashed in the coverage of sports? Are Americans afraid of China? Is Russia now considered unimportant enough so we can bash it in a very unsportsmanlike fashion these Winter Games? Do we see in faded Russia our own diminishing might and are we engaged in self-loathing and mutilation?

As I write this, I am hoping that my good kind of patriotism will emerge before the Games end. Sweden has not yet played all of its hockey games and of course I hope that Sweden will win gold in hockey. But if Sweden does not win gold, and if the United States misses out as well, will this have been our winter of Russian bashing as we celebrated the coming together of different peoples from all over the world in the "spirit" of the Olympics? ☛

The "Sinful" Ingmar Bergman

The other night I decided to take in some Bergman. I had a few choices, thanks to Amazon's instant video streaming service. It made it possible for me to avoid my old standby, *The Seventh Seal* (*Det sjunde inseglet*). While it does feature a young, gaunt and very Nordic looking Max von Sydow, whose hair appears blond and lit like a fire even in black-and-white, after my hectic week at work, a scene of him playing chess against Death with a capital D or people dying from the bubonic plague was not necessarily the stimulating intellectual fare I had in mind.

Imagine how delighted I was to come across *Summer with Monika* (*Sommaren med Monika*). What an idyllic title and how beautiful it sounds in Swedish. In addition, frankly, remembering from years back the stills of the lovely and voluptuous Harriet Anderson as Monika in the nude against the backdrop of the sea and an island, both the reptilian part of my brain and its more reasoning areas were in a receptive mode.

I should have known that Ingmar Bergman would not disappoint. Even my wife, who upon learning that I was going to watch one of his films, was not disappointed, as she retreated to the other end of the house with the dogs and catalogs and a home improvement show on the television. She soon announced, while I turned down the volume, "I can hear lots of Swedish angst screaming!"

"Well, that's just how he is," I said, almost feeling the need to defend Ingmar Bergman for not having worked on *Saturday Night Live!* or producing *Scooby-Doo*.

I don't know why I had expected Bergman to produce something that was not full of pain, disappointment, with maybe only a moment or pinch of hope. *Sommaren med Monika* is a 1953 film, made when Bergman was young, so why should it have had peace and beauty, even the healing power of love, as offered by the more recent films of Woody Allen, a great admirer and, by his own admission, student of Bergman's work. At least Woody Allen's early works display a sense of humor that is neither biting nor cruel.

Sommaren med Monika offers a love story of two young persons. Monika needs no further introduction. The male character, with the unlikely name of Harry Lund, is played by Lars Ekborg. Harry Lund has a very boyish, almost pretty, and innocent look, and his hands tremble when a very assertive Monika asks him to light her cigarette in a dreary bar. She approaches Harry with an aggressiveness that today would earn her the title of "man-eater." Wonder how she came across to film audiences in the 1950s?

The two escape their dead-end jobs and unsatisfying home lives by motor-boating to a world of islands so lovely in the Swedish summer. Dialogue early on is idyllic in a way that unfortunately turns even the most kind and optimistic filmgoer into a snarky observer. The manner in which the couple carries on about the man getting an education so the two can buy a house and have a child while the woman stays at home, would make even the most ardent Palme hater hiss with disgust. Bergman manages to ruin any kind of good memories we might have of youthful idealism or loving support of such we might muster. How cruel and sarcastic Bergman is!

The clouds in *Sommaren med Monika* are a recurring tableau, watchable without a soundtrack, even as they heavy-handedly spell out trouble in paradise. And how hard to tune out that we are being told the couple is on a journey when toward the beginning of the film we are shown the motor boat owned by Harry's father running through bridge after bridge to escape the city and civilization.

We must also forgive Bergman for rendering it as if he were stage and prop master intent on not remaining invisible when we watch Monika becoming savage in the absence of civilization as she steals a roast and begins to eat it like an animal. Then there is the almost-killing that the author of *Lord of the Flies* would be proud of.

Since this is a Bergman film so joy and beauty must not be allowed to rule, the couple returns to civilization. And what a paradise it is not. Monika is pregnant, Harry has to get a job that is still not fun, and what money he brings home to Monika is not enough.

Monika makes this very clear. The story continues with the noble Harry trying to study and quiet the screaming baby while Monika does nothing to help the couple build their future together.

Harry, as directed by Bergman, appears a puppet of good, and one can only wonder if Bergman wants us to suffer while we watch the good man suffer or if he wants us to help Harry grow a spine and take action to put an end to his suffering. Monika is a bitch and whore the way Bergman depicts her (I choose these words to convey tone compliments of Bergman and not because I want to use bad language), as she sleeps around while good Harry exists only to show suffering. Even the most diehard feminist could be turned into a man's rights activist, if there is such a role.

On the other hand, is Ingmar Bergman's portrayal of Monika a once-in-a-lifetime situational sketch? Can we understand and forgive Bergman the artist for perhaps using the film as a therapeutic vehicle for Bergman the man? Many of us know, either from personal experience or from friends whose relationships have ended badly, that anger, even bitterness has its unfortunate place in the lives of human beings. Can we forgive Bergman's heavy-handed moving of the pieces across his chessboard of a film because it is the work of a young filmmaker? Is the lens through which we view *Sommaren med Monika* today clouded by experiences of a world so different from the 1950s that we fail to laud Ingmar Bergman for having created something that was indeed artful when the film first appeared? Do we need to make any excuses for Bergman the artist or man?

When and where will we – Swedes, Swedish-Americans, citizens of the globe – watch Ingmar Bergman films? Will his work endure – and more so than simply as a national treasure or monument that is only visited dutifully or not at all? When is the last time you watched an Ingmar Bergman film? Should Swedish school children watch Bergman's work? Will they watch it or is Bergman yet another dying giant who in our current generation is dead on arrival?

As Bergman wrote on a note to his housekeeper, *"Om den här osten är Jarlslberg är jag Kalle Anka!"* ("If this cheese is Jarlsberg, I'm Donald Duck!") Perhaps we have lost our artistic taste buds and ability to appreciate anything that deviates from safe staples. ♟

"Keep Cool but Care"

Christmas is the time of year when we so much desire peace, and ironically so many of us dash faster than Santa's reindeer and his overworked elves to make that peace happen. Even if we engage in our hunt for presents by making purchases online, this happens when eyes, hands and necks are tired from working at the computer during the day and we maximize one more moment of time by ordering from our iPads while streaming episodes of *Welcome to Sweden*.

Faith tugs at the sleeves of some of us. No matter how secular we have become, even as we try to tune out Christmas music blaring like non-biblical trumpets at us, there is a bit of Lutheran in all of us. Who does not remember, at the very least, the Bible or Book of Psalms we had as children? That children's Bible with illustrations to make some of the more dramatic moments come alive: Moses parting the sea, David and Goliath going at it.

I hope there is a bit of David in us; I know there is. Not only to face the crises of the world, which extend into and across borders – whether we live in Sweden, Ukraine or on the continent of Africa.

Much has been said and done in the name of religion through the centuries. I am not going to blame my early years of Lutheran influences for this, the habits, the familiarity of particular objects and rituals. The lighting of a candle each weekend, the procession of *Sankta Lucia*, the opening of the doors of the Advent calendar, even opening gifts on *julafton* (Christmas Eve) as opposed to the American tradition of getting up in the morning on Christmas day to open presents. It is dim but lighting up more and more – like my mother taking me to *julotta*, in what was a religious as well as secular experience of the holiday.

It is time to make peace with that part of my experience, and I am sure other Swedes have similar quarrels within themselves. One way to find peace is to embrace some of the traditions and their relationship to our religious upbringing.

But in making this choice, in order to find stillness, try to avoid some of the commercialism. There is nothing wrong with acquiring an exciting new gadget, but how beautiful the vision of the Christmas tree, decorated simply or even very visually elaborate, with the traditional Swedish paper heart baskets. Wrap just a few presents and see if they can be given – and received – without extra adornment.

Fellow Kindle and other portable electronic users: I am not going to ask you to abandon these devices and go through some kind of detox during the holiday; this would not make for peace. But let there be a book, yes, one made of paper, with glue and print, a spine that you at first take care not to bend but then give up, inside one of the simply wrapped presents.

And as you no doubt have feasted your eyes on so many photos of delicious Christmas food already, make it a bit simpler for yourself and your family, and sit down to just a few favorites and enjoy them.

This talk of peace is not to say you should begin to disengage from the world. Even those of us who have those intentions, don't manage to live up to such expectations of solipsism or non-involvement – nor would we really want to, whether or not we're religious. There is a good Samaritan in all of us that will come out, whether you are Lutheran or an atheist, or any number of labels we are so fond of using as a human race, labels which unfortunately so often cause discord.

No, "*nu är det jul igen*," and yes, it can be a bit hectic like that song and dancing around the Christmas tree, but try to limit such frenzy to an intentional musical interlude without knocking the tree down, and for next year "keep cool but care," as Benny Profane, one of the characters of Thomas Pynchon's novel *Gravity's Rainbow* said. Gravitas for the holiday, gravitas for the new year. *Good Jul* everyone! 🐦

Glögg and Julskinka. Okay, but Stjärngosse?

Wet wool socks. I am standing in my grandmother's vestibule, a very sizeable room to leave off your coats and shoes. At my young and clumsy age I have not noticed until it's too late the invasion of wet snow from huge adult shoes pooling onto my feet inside wool socks.

It could be worse and it is. I am a *stjärngosse*, wearing my father's white dress shirt as a gown and I have a cone-shaped, tall hat on my head that does not feel very steady. Then I have to keep track of a stick with a golden star attached to it, a lollipop that cannot go into the mouth. The things they do to little boys who still need to learn to tie shoes and tell time!

But I know this is a very important occasion, on this day of *Sankta Lucia* – to visit my *mormor* because my independent mother, who usually does not take orders or kindly so from her own mother, does not want any fuss today and it is clear we must go and make our visit. Yes, my little brother is in tow also, but at my age he doesn't matter. Besides, my grandmother will give me all the attention.

Not exactly Christmas sentiments, but I am sure I am not the only Swedish boy to have felt this way. Nor the only one who had to wear his father's dress shirt (likely an old one with a hole for some event that borders on the holy) instead of having a costume sewn for the occasion. I felt poor and slighted for not having a custom-made costume. I also did not like that all the fuss was made over a blond girl with candles in her hair. I really did not know anything about this celebration, other than I had to wear a stupid outfit, a girl with lots of candles in her hair got all the attention and I was pushed to visit my grandmother, whom I normally begged and loved to visit.

It was probably the costume that was making me grouchy during this Christmas time event. To this day I don't like to wear costumes. Even if it means champagne and adults losing their inhibitions as if a little mask would the trick.

This is supposed to be a Christmas column, about celebrating Christmas in Sweden or doing it the Swedish way. I must summon some happy memories (note to all Swedes: summon happy Christmas memories). And I must forget about the Christmas column I wrote last year, about Santa Claus and Jesus at the mall. Thank God that one did not make it into *Nordstjernan* – it would really have put a damper on the holiday season and filled publisher Ulf Barslund Mårtensson's mailbag with lumps of coal, I mean heated correspondence.

Actually I do have many happy memories of Christmas in Sweden and Swedish Christmas celebrations, but in the interest of full disclosure I thought I must share the good, the bad and the ugly.

Julskinka is what was so beautiful about Christmas in Sweden. Just looking at the specially prepared ham, seeing the breading on the outside, along with just the right sliver of fat – I am definitely a fan of Swedish Christmas and thank the porkers that continue to make it possible!

I think one of the advantages of the Swedish Christmas is that we have *lilla julafton* and also *julafton*. Getting a present on the 23rd of December is great. Why put it off until the 25th. Even better is the Swedish custom of celebrating *julafton* on the 24th, at night. It happens at a time when young and old, early and late risers alike, are awake and can enjoy exchanging gifts. It is lovely not to see or smell family members and relatives au naturel. It is amazing how the more puritanical Americans share the way they look when they just wake up, have not yet brushed their teeth or taken a shower in their celebration of Christmas on the morning of December 25. In addition, why torture little children by having them wait so long for their presents. Give them the pardon of a Swedish *lille julafton*!

What I really enjoyed about our Swedish Christmas was having a *jultomte* (Santa Claus) who distributed the gifts from a sack, and as we grew a little older, retrieved the gifts from around the tree. It wasn't that I believed in Santa Claus – even during my formative years as a tortured *stjärngosse* I could tell it was my uncle behind the badly taped cotton beard, donned quickly after the evening meal like indigestion. And the year my grandfather was a *tomte* (as in *jultomte*), I think my very young and little brother could have spotted him as a nonmythological creature right away. But that was the fun of it – silly adults!

I liked having the *jultomte* officiating over the ceremony because he distributed the gifts in a way that created anticipation, right then and there, while gift-recipients-in-waiting, with bellies full, digested and listened for the next name to be called out. To this day, I prefer this Swedish gift distribution practice over the American one which I have observed to consist of everyone diving into their pile or stash, with feigned and faint interest in others' gifts after-the-fact. Of course I am not saying that I was really interested as a child if my father received a razor or my brother got new clothes (or if I received new clothes for that matter). But the anticipation created by *jultomten* slowly giving out presents is laudatory, as much as the welfare state steadily giving is repulsive (see, I have to sneak in something ugly along with the good).

On a serious note, whether you celebrate Christmas in Sweden, in America, anywhere on the globe, if you are Swedish, have Swedish relatives or family, or are generation X to the Xth power Swedish descendant and really know nothing about Sweden, a Swedish Christmas is worth celebrating.

It comes, as do all Christmases, during a time of the year when expectations have been turned up to an incredibly high volume. Even if we know we should ignore this volume, it is very difficult to do so. By now and in this issue you have read all sorts of great ideas that can make Christmas Swedish and beautiful. Don't stress over having to make every kind of dish imaginable and making everything look as beautiful as in *Nordstjernan*'s photos. Instead, choose one item, more if you are a holiday masochist, and take some time this season and really enjoy the item. As you eat *julskinka* or open the door to an Advent calendar, be in the moment. Give yourself the gift of contemplation or daydreaming. Even if it means remembering the indignities of being a *stjärngosse*.

This has been your *skribent*, hoping for new blue felt tip pens, wishing you a God Jul! And an even better *Gott Nytt År*. ❧

Musings on, of and by a "Certified Swede"

It is with some trepidation that I approach the subject "Certified Swedish." You see, the words of my mother throughout the years still come up today: "*Lagom är bäst!*" To give her credit for practicing this philosophy of life stated so beautifully and untranslatable from Swedish is to give the saying exact meaning: My mother is "certifiably Swedish" with the tone of voice she uses when saying "*Lagom är bäst*" and because she doesn't say it with an exclamation mark at the end. This practice makes my mother certifiably Swedish.

But we are not here to make my mother certifiably Swedish, however worthy she is of such a citation. I mention my mother's wisdom because of a very real fear I have – from my experiences living in America – that we might have people who now want to be not only certifiably Swedish but The Most Certifiably Swedish. People will overdo it. While Swedes are certainly not immune to wanting to be champions and the best, if they become such, they manifest their status in a more understated way than Swedes or Swedish-Americans who have lived in America for almost any length of time.

The best thing – or maybe worst – would be to see someone certifiably Swedish like this: Mr. X, who has lived in the U.S. his entire life and knows he is of Swedish origin suddenly decides to go "whole hog" to be certifiably Swedish. While up until this point the only thought he has given Sweden has been the Swedish Bikini Team, Mr. X goes shopping at IKEA and replaces his ranch house furniture and decorations with everything "IKEA." Out goes the table that is round and made with a limestone top covered by glass. In comes the new coffee table, complemented by square end tables, monochromatic and wooden. Down with the Texas longhorns displayed over the fireplace. That print with the Swedish alphabet is a wonderful substitute. And while he's at it, Mr. X stocks his freezer with Swedish meatballs and eats those five or six times a week instead of the steak he has been used to consuming.

No, going to IKEA is not a recommended way to "go Swedish" and in the process become certifiably Swedish. While IKEA has some wonderful Swedish furniture, the sanctity of becoming and being certifiably Swedish would be violated if Mr. X thought he could be a "certified Swede" by importing props and scenery from Sweden.

Frightful, too, it would be to see Ms. X decide to color her hair blond, in a step toward becoming certifiably Swedish. Yes, not all Swedes are blond, nor do they remain blond. Filling her shopping bags or online cart with Dala horses, trolls, Carl Larsson prints, commemorative items related to the Swedish royals – this kind of instant transformation fulfilled by commerce is not an acceptable approach, if they want to be certifiably Swedish.

Well, if I can't buy my way into Swedish-ness or Swede-dom, how do I stand a chance of being certifiably Swedish? One more acceptable way would be to pursue becoming certifiably Swedish through education. In a feverish dream, I recently imagined candidates traveling to New Canaan, Connecticut – the limo ride from JFK airport – to be dropped off at a huge building that looks like an old Hollywood studio, complete with soundstage. Candidates of the "*Nordstjernan* Academy of Swedish Certification" would immediately be whisked into the giant building. Inside is a giant theme park with Swedish lakes, summer cottages and persons dressed in regional costumes; dialects could be heard floating over streams filled with trout and pike, including those of seagulls shrieking overhead along the simulated coastline.

I return to the grounding words of my mother: "*Lagom är bäst.*" Following her wisdom and path, I say that to become certifiably Swedish, a gradual discovery of Swedish-ness is essential. It can be a detail, such as realizing when you cut a block of cheese with a knife you feel some guilt because you are not using the *osthyvel* that you never thought you could live without when you first came to America. Or, as a Swedish-American, you might come across the *osthyvel* in a store and bring it home and find you really like using it. This is one step toward becoming certifiably Swedish – the simple act of preparing cheese for your sandwich, the "how" indicative of much more, showing the "who" you are.

Have you found yourself cheering for the Swedes during the Olympics, or at the very least being happy when Swedes win? Have you found a place in your heart for Sweden and America? Yes, whether you like it or not, you are on your way to the medal podium of being certifiably Swedish.

And did you enjoy strong coffee before Starbucks made America's heartbeat go up and skip wholesale? Another mental check mark in your certifiably Swedish notebook or memo to Siri. You decide whether this memo is in English, Swedish or Swenglish.

Now stop reading – on second thought, with a nod to my editor and friend Ulf Barslund Mårtensson, don't stop reading until you have finished the whole issue of *Nordstjernan*. But then go out into the world and come back with experiences, lingonberry-finger imprints of your Swedish-ness, recording your daily journey of becoming certifiably Swedish, or being certifiably Swedish, as you ride your Dala horse like a knight with the tip of your lance offering the credo, "*Lagom är bäst.*" And yes, it is more than perfectly alright if someone sees the Swedish flag flutter in the wind atop your helmet. And who knows, they also might see on it a "Certified Swedish" sticker. ☙

"My Lawn is my Castle"

Last night it rained, water pouring deeply into the ground, and while I was happy to see all the flowers and plants stand up after lying low to protect themselves during more than seven weeks of "water, what's that," I felt a special joy in my lawn transforming itself before my eyes.

I don't know how rain accomplishes what watering by humans cannot. It is a miracle worker, catching up in one day the unwatered lawn to its spoiled neighbor that had a steady stream of sprinkler system watering sessions several times a week.

I do not have a sprinkler system. I'll admit I have had fantasies about having a sprinkler system. Not necessarily because I don't want to spend my time lugging hoses when the lawn really needs water, but because the lawns with artificial water-aids look so much greener than my own lawn, and I feel the pain of my lawn when it gets too dry. Yes, I relate to my lawn. Lest you think this strange, I am sure there are others who can relate to the relationship I have with my lawn.

There is an old saying about a man's home being his castle – no doubt a very politically incorrect statement these days. Well then, if a person's home is his castle, then the lawn is a source of hubris with pride that is not the bad kind of those persons who value lawn.

To me the way a person's lawn looks says something about that person. If you have a lawn that is neatly mowed but not edged, with annoying spillage onto the concrete barrier laid out by municipality, that is a statement. It is not a statement showing your independence and letting your hair down. It is a statement of character, amounting to being a neglectful person and not caring that other neighbors, such as myself, will have to look at the horrid haircut of green you parade before your house. It is you and your sloth on display for all to suffer and see.

Likewise, if you let a few tall strands of weeds or a different kind of grass stand on a lawn that is otherwise not in need of mowing, that decision shows you do not care to keep some semblance of order in your life.

Now if you don't water, that makes you for the most part someone who is a conservator of precious natural resources, but there comes also the time when it is essential to stop your lawn's suffering, when the grass gets crinkly and you leave your footprint on it like an astronaut on the moon. You must carry the overpriced, green plastic sprinkler to strategic spots on your lawn and water, where nature is dehydrating your lawn.

By now you have surmised that I think a lot about lawns and have a relationship with my lawn that many people likely do not. I would venture a guess that most people who employ a lawn service do not have an intimate relationship with their lawn. Some people say they don't have time to mow the lawn, but I would counter they prefer not to make time to have a relationship with their lawn. Some people say their allergies act up when they mow the lawn. Well, I sneeze at that statement. My allergies come into full bloom, but that does not mean I am going to give up mowing the lawn. Allergies can be had by most people whether they mow a lawn or not.

This whole mowing-your-own-lawn versus hiring-a-lawn-service thing crystallizes the relationship between a person and his lawn. Moreover, the way a person of a lawn service mows the lawn is a portrait of a person's relationship with a lawn.

Allow me to come full circle to where we began with rain this morning after a dry spell. Before I left for work I retrieved two sticks from my wife's planting area (she was not using them) and inserted them into my lawn (forgive me, lawn). I wrote with a Sharpie permanent marker in capital letters DO NOT MOW on multipurpose office paper, inserted it into a see-through folder (compliments of my wife's orderly office stash), and attached it to the sticks so the end result was a kind of cross, letting the lawn service person who mows my neighbor's lawn know not to enter with his huge riding mower on the thickest tires I have ever seen. That's right, KEEP OUT.

You see, this lawn service person, for years - in order to quickly reach one spot of my neighbor's lawn - has crossed the border onto my lawn, with the result that I have a strip that gets mowed by him, compressed to lie deeper than the rest of my lawn. This uncaring mower has also exposed roots of my neighbor's beautiful trees, simply because the lawn service person cares only about speed and ease of mowing.

And I had just carefully repaired that section of lawn, restoring it to what it was before greedy big machine mower man minced it.

My wife, who is a very compassionate person, points out that if I had a lawn service I would be in a hurry also, because that is how I would make my living, i.e., the quicker I mow, the more lawns I cut, and the more revenue I take in.

I disagree. I would mow the lawns with love, not with the furor and disrespect that this lawn service person shows in his very impersonal relationship with lawns. Another person who mows lawns for a living, and whom I have known for 18 years in his business, mows slower, with care, and you know by just watching the way his body moves, that his mowing is the act of loving caretaking.

So the business of lawn mowing is no different from the business of any other business or activity. People reveal much about their relationship with others and their surroundings by the way they go about, yes, repetition intentional, their business.

I am hoping you will weigh in on this issue, whether your allergies are acting up from having just come in from mowing or you feel a slight headache coming on from having paid your lawn service. Or maybe you slice deli meat in a shop you own, thinking this will be a nice, tasty sandwich for your customers, or you want to get the food served so you can get your check, close up the store and finish mopping before you go home.

Awaiting your comments, and be kind to your lawn! ♥

Oh, the Story I Found!

My *morfar* (grandfather on my mother's father) hunted alligators by a lake in Småland. If this sounds strange to you, imagine how my mother must have felt when, as a child in the 1940s in Sweden, she read *Pelle Svanslös i Amerika*. Or for that matter, how strange and incredible a journey to America Gösta Knutsson's book, published in 1943, would have been to any Swedish youngster.

For several years now I have kept a stack of Pelle Svanslös adventures on my bookshelf. My mother gave them to me in the process of downsizing and no doubt wanting to make sure they were in good hands, as she is advancing in age. I treasure these books because they must have made a lasting impression on my mother. She loves to talk about Pelle and that evil Måns and his stupid followers Bill and Bull. When she mentions them it is with an intensity not given any other book talks we have had.

Until two weeks ago I had never read any of the Pelle Svanslös books, not even as a child. My reading list back in Sweden consisted of *Emil i Lönneberga, Karlsson på Taket, Pippi Långstrump, Ture Sventon Privatdetektiv* and *Nils Holgersson* – add to that Tintin, Kalle Anka and Fantomen, while not Swedish characters, certainly adopted as if homegrown by me and many other children in Sweden.

"Oh the story that I found," to paraphrase Dr. Seuss deliberately as badly, when I opened up *Pelle Svanslös i Amerika* on a recent trip. You have heard the saying "I could not put it down," and it was one of those rare occasions when I kept reading; I was fortunate to have the time to do so. Gösta Knutsson, presumably writing for children, immediately drew me into his world of cats that behaved and appeared as if they were persons, while existing in a world that features, at least peripherally, people, and also showed the cats, both in print and lovely illustrations, to be cats.

Gösta Knutsson has the ability to write in a way that appeals to all age levels, including those reaching middle age, such as myself. He also has the ability to tell of things that concern society and the adult world, without being heavy-handed. At no time does one feel he is creating a moralistic fable, so with all due respect to George Orwell and his *Animal Farm*, move over George, Gösta is the champ. Hands down, Gösta wins the match! Gösta is the Ingemar Johansson of prose as it relates to animals, entertainment and literature. And T.S. Eliot, with your cats and subsequent mega musical machine, I'm sorry – nice try, but, if you will excuse the phrase, you are not the cat's meow.

I mentioned earlier how strange this Pelle Svanslös book must have seemed to a Swedish child, maybe an adult also, in the early 1940s. I wonder how many in Sweden really knew anything at all about events or details as Knutsson depicts them in Pelle's adventure across the vast ocean.

Knutsson informs us that America has lots of automobiles and skyscrapers. But this is where the familiarity ends for what most in Sweden in 1943 would have known. He tells us that in America there is an ice cream man on nearly every corner because Americans are terribly fond of ice cream. Elevators in America are 10 times as fast as those in Sweden. He teaches his readers what a "drug" store is, and depicts a counter where Americans sit on high stools and drink something sweet, and eat ice cream and fried eggs.

We also learn about gangsters. In this book they are ever present and while no blood is spilled, their actions and behavior should scare any child beyond what they might see today watching *The Sopranos*, *Good Fellas*, or any mobster offering on television. Without wishing to spoil the book, I think I can share that it is both frightful and hilarious to have the cat gangsters raise their paws and shout in unison several times the abbreviation of their gang, G.G. (for "Gangster Gang") and motto, "Everything Ours!"

As part of the story and Pelle's encounters, Knutsson depicts interesting social behavior such as Swedish cats immigrating to America and changing their names to sound American, as well as Swedish cats having various language proficiencies in Swedish, leaving the old country behind and inevitably losing touch with *gamla Sverige*. He manages to entertain and instruct in such instances, and only twice in the book occurs an overt pedagogical lesson, that would these days be called a "teaching moment." They concern race relations. I translate in the passage below from page 83 of the 1947 edition of *Pelle Svanslös i Amerika*:

Pelle is told by another cat, "But you should not buy [a souvenir]
from him, because he is a Negro [cat]." Pelle's response is
a manifesto against racism, "If I could only understand why it should
matter if a cat is a Negro or not. As long as he is a good cat,
that's what matters. If he is evil, that is so much worse than
a Negro cat who is good, and if I am good, I am not one iota better
than a Negro cat who is good. If a Negro cat is evil, he is just like
any other cat who is evil. Whether the nose is black or white
shouldn't matter."

I wonder how much Swedish children or Swedes in the early 1940s knew about racism in America or what the opinions of the Swedish people were.

Following Pelle on his adventure in America we are in good hands with Gösta Knutsson, who educates us about geography and different cities, and even includes a tour of the Swedish exhibit that has brought Pelle and his human companions to America in the first place. The chapter features a beautiful drawing of a giant *dalahäst* a boy has managed to climb to ride, as another child photographs the moment and Pelle and another cat look on. Even birch trees have been brought to the exhibit. Good to know Swedish marketing and public relations were at work in America in the 1940s.

Having had two weeks to think about *Pelle Svanslös i Amerika*, my hope is that by introducing or reintroducing you to the Swedish cat and his creator Gösta Knutsson you will visit or revisit some of his work. More than anything, I would like to hear from those of you who were alive in the 1940s and read Pelle Svanslös books, your perceptions of America back then, inside or outside the Bonniers Barnbibliotek book covers of a great Swedish cat.

It is important for the sake of Swedish and Swedish-American history to know how and how much perceptions have changed as the countries of Sweden and America both integrate and disintegrate in a world that is, as they say – whether you like it or not – global. *Tack ska du ha!* 🐾

My Swedish Crime Drama

I've been thinking about shooting a Swedish crime series. Speaking of shooting, there won't be any, except maybe at the end, and that's only to satisfy American audiences. I will have a heroine who looks depressed, is pale and has blonde hair, but she will be really good looking and mysterious in her absence of makeup. She has lines under her eyes and her hairstyle must be simple to maintain also. Even I as a man who knows nothing about that sort of stuff recognize this attractive simplicity.

Like a bed whenever there is any sex, my crime show will be shown briefly, in the dark, alluded to, and you can forget about any nudity unless it's when she gets up afterward. Swedish women have a cool way of getting out of bed or moving around in bed and actually showing their breasts. I have always wondered why women in America hold up their bed sheets as if some guy in the room was delivering pizza.

My Swedish crime series will have lots of people who speak as if they are from Stockholm and the north of Sweden. It doesn't matter if the story is set in the south, in which people have a very distinctive way of drawing out words, just as in America. Speaking of accents, my crime show will have some moments where Swedish characters speak English as matter-of-factly as if they were driving a car that looks small enough for clowns at the circus, which they often do. They, the Swedes, will speak English with just a hint of song in their pronunciation, not even getting into Muppet Chef territory if Dick Cheney bit them in the ass. But all this accent appreciation, like wincing when foreign terrorists or crime figures in the Swedish crime series speak Swedish with a foreign accent – that is for true language aficionados, the kind of people who read Shouts & Murmurs in the *New Yorker*.

You are never going to see any of my Swedish crime drama Swedes eat typical Swedish fare, except maybe crayfish if it is an episode set in the summer. People expect that, and the food is just close and palatable enough to lobsters and other seafood devoured in the American market. Yes, I know what you are thinking. Where is the *lutfisk*? Sorry to disappoint, this is my Swedish crime drama and these days no self-respecting Swede would be caught dead eating lutefisk as it is called in America. Speaking of which again, death by *lutfisk* might be a good idea. Maybe not directly as part of the plot but as an insert when a character watches a television programme. Yes, it will be a programme, to get the flavor right, not a program.

My Swedish crime series will have the usual blue and yellow police car paint scheme and the officers will also show their colors and I know it will just amaze American viewers how civilized the police appear, even dainty. They don't draw their guns very often and if they seem powerful in a menacing way it will be toward journalists or common bystanders. The crooks are treated with respect.

The crime drama will be in separate movies, not episodes, even if they could be episodes of a drama. The closing credits will feature all sorts of neat names like Björn and Ulf and be so intriguing viewers will want to watch them roll, even if they are white on black background while a loud and depressing score finishes off the film, yes, the film.

You will see many women in positions of authority in my Swedish crime drama, and these women, too, will wear minimal make-up by American standards. Many of them will be middle-aged with wrinkles showing, but have a beauty that is radiating, no, not like the summer solstice, and we will see them let their hair down some time during the episode (that is as in loosening the bun or braid so the hair can fall shoulder-length).

Men in the show will be either power hungry, corrupt or inept and occasionally the good looking guy women decide to hop in the sack with. This seems to be some kind of universal portrayal of men, in my Swedish crime drama and probably even in Kenya (we just don't get to see Kenyan crime drama on television).

What else have I left out of my Swedish crime drama? It doesn't really matter because the plot will be either about some religious fanatic (homegrown weird Swede, Calvinist streaking), a narcotics syndicate, a kidnapper of children, a rapist or the popular, bottom-of-the-barrel corrupt politician.

That is not a very wide range but we are not watching the Swedish crime drama for a wide range. Just cut to sad, sonorous music, roll those opening credits with *ö*'s and *ä*'s, a dark afternoon or darker evening (just all the same, as it is always dark in Sweden unless it's that well-publicized lit summer), show the blonde heroine with lines on her face despite and because of being young and attractive, and let ring out "*fan,*" "*djävlar,*" and other curse words in Swedish, because those peaceful Swedes have all sorts of nasty stuff coming from their jaws, unless they pause for a drink somewhere, or, more likely, have the weight of their life talk to them in shouts and murmurs while drinking large quantities of hard liquor, and lately, white wine.

I will not end this piece about my Swedish crime drama with *skål*, but I might consider doing so if the series satisfies the voracious appetite of Americans and I can come over here and work with you and not pay the taxes we Swedes are so famous for offering and taking. *Hej då!* That's "bye" to you, but you would already know that from watching so much Swedish crime television, I mean film. ❧

NOT Certifiably Swedish!

I can hear him now, the Swedish Chef, making sounds that are supposedly Swedish.

I have never been able to imitate this Muppet's speech, but that is perhaps because I am Swedish and this character is certifiably NOT Swedish.

And the way he carries on, knife in one hand, chicken in the other, the connection between knife and head chopped off all too clear. This is not to say that I, as a Swedish American, don't like to eat chicken or think that chickens peacefully and magically appear, aesthetically converted on my plate. But is this really the kind of role model we need to put before our children's eyes?

Besides, the Swedish Chef moves his hands in a way that is deliberately spastic – as if he is making fun of persons who might have medical issues. Yes, the Swedish Chef is definitively, absolutely, NOT certifiably Swedish. And were these Viking times, we could proclaim loudly, "The Swedish Chef Must Die!" Then we'd have to clean our sword, or at least take an honest whack at the chicken – none of that trembling, jerking, will-he-kill-the-chicken-or-not pose, with incomprehensible mumbling that is definitely NOT Swedish.

Now that we have recovered from a gruesome fright-fest in the spirit of Halloween and decapitating that annoying "Swedish" Muppet, let us make a list of more candidates who do not represent Sweden in a favorable light, and so, no Valhalla for them!

Clearly the father of Emil (i Lönneberga) must be taken to court and serve some time in a cushy Swedish prison. After all, locking your child in a shed and being an early purveyor of child labor – having Emil produce piece-meal wooden figure after wooden figure – will not do at all.

While we take our walk through the annals of fictive characters brought to life in various artistic media, the wonderful portrayal by Krister Henriksson of the Swedish detective Kurt Wallander must no longer find its substitute in Kenneth Branagh's portrayal of the same character. Branagh is so UN-SWEDISH in the way he looks into the camera, posing to give us a look that signals like a traffic light, "I am crazy, Swedish, depressed." Not to say that non-Swedes could not play a Swedish character, but Branagh's Kurt Wallander is definitely NOT certifiably Swedish. But I know this will not keep my wife from preferring the Branagh impersonation.

And the Swedish Bikini Team? A sex-in-your-face marketing idea with an artifice about these ladies does not qualify them to be certifiably Swedish. The sense of humor appears to have been forgotten with this "team," or it is not a Swedish sense of humor.

I have held back on Pippi (does she really need a last name at this point anymore?), wondering how willing I am to take cover. Pippi is self-reliant, metes out her own justice, certainly does not allow herself to be held captive by any Swedish child protective services or their notions, and what is she doing clothing a monkey? No, Pippi is not rule- or law-abiding enough to be certifiably Swedish. She is not quite on the same non-conformist level as the violent berserker Vikings, but how would she fit into Swedish society in 2013? Perhaps that is why we like her so much? It really pains me to have to disqualify Pippi from the Certified Swedish bunch.

Could you imagine Olof Palme riding atop Gubben with Pippi? I am sure Palme could imagine himself doing so. But Olof Palme was a real person – there is no denying that, though some would probably not grant him that much. However, the fictive construct of Olof Palme is certainly very non-Swedish. To take a whole people and subjugate them, transform them into something in his mind's image is certifiably very non-Swedish and unbecoming. Certainly not "live and let live." The title of a James Bond film comes more to mind.

I hope that some of the following Swedish fictive characterizations will also die. To set the record straight:

1. All Swedes are not exhibitionists who like to walk around naked any chance they get. Swedish women do not all sunbathe without a top on.

2. All Swedes are not atheists or worshippers of Thor and company. Many Swedes believe in God, even if they do not attend church.

3. All Swedes are not *sambo* types (no, I am not talking about the children's book). Swedes actually do get married and do not always live together in a *sambo* situation.

4. All Swedes are not alcoholics who get drunk every Friday or Saturday night to the point of crawling on all fours and blacking out. Many Swedes enjoy wine and drink it in moderation, even during the week. They do not all save up for a giant vodka bender on the weekend, for example.

5. All Swedes are not depressed. There are a remarkable number of Swedes who are quite content, dare we say it, happy, and also cheerful. Get to know a cheerful Swede today!

6. All Swedes are not blonde. No, I won't get into how you determine that.

7. All Swedes are not socialists. Really. There is a whole spectrum of political beliefs.

8. All Swedish boys do not play ice hockey at the age of 3. Or 4, 5, 6 and so on. Swedes are great hockey players, but just as in America not everyone is cut out to be a football- or baseball player, some Swedish boys take up other pursuits that will leave them with a whole set of teeth. By the way, it is also a false stereotype that Swedish ice hockey players, or hockey players of any nationality, don't have a real set of teeth.

The list of uncertifiably Swedish traits or characterizations is long as the day and light can be short in Sweden. While writing this column I was visited, even haunted by another set of contradictions – that it is not certifiably Swedish to create a list of exclusions. To allay my Swedish guilt I thought for a moment of including a few constructs that are certifiably Swedish. But then I felt a sense of Swedish honesty tug at my wrist and decided, fellow Swedes and citizens of the world, I owe it to you as a Swede to be honest and finish on this topic alone, however uncomfortable and Swedish doing so might make me feel. ♛

Broadening Horizons

With the exception of a few grouchy people –
the ones we half-playfully say should crawl back
under the rock from where they came or into their
poorly insulated *sommarstuga* – most will answer
yes, from experience or didactic echo: Travel does
broaden the mind. I can hear also my Swedish
parents say this, and while I only half understood
what they meant, taken out of my Lego world, I can
report that they made sure my brother and I got
to experience firsthand a foreign culture: America.

Back when we traveled to America, it was considered very extravagant and/or somewhat nutty to cross the vast ocean from Sweden by airplane and spend several weeks in a land most people only knew as larger than life, and not necessarily in a positive way, from what they had heard or imagined from popular media. And back then popular media meant a newspaper made of paper, a magazine and some coverage from one television station broadcasting a few hours a day, supplemented by transistor radio broadcasts. Believe it or not, I am talking about 1970, months after Americans had landed on the moon.

Our parents succeeded in broadening our minds family spent two summers exploring America. And explore we did, spending endless hours in a rental car going from coast to coast, but especially spending time in the "west," compliments of my father's great interest in the old west and cowboy movies. Yes, *High Chaparral*, *The Virginian*, and the occasional John Wayne movie were ours for the taking in Sweden and my father was taken indeed.

I am not sure my mind was broadened the way my parents had intended, however. I recall that we reached the Grand Canyon, something which was supposed to be famous. Just before we were to get out and marvel at the wonder, the front of my father's pants somehow split. He was very embarrassed by this fact and it did not make it any easier that my brother and I, and, truth be known, my mother, thought this was a hilarious occasion. So all I remember from this wonder of the world is my father grabbing the cowboy hat he had bought and holding it in front of his pants, making his way to the railing of the Grand Canyon in a snaking way, or as if he had injured himself walking. As a side note, this was before the term "sciatica" had become all the rage and every adult was afflicted by its flare-ups.

Tombstone, Arizona. It was supposed to be very interesting. We were in a sandy graveyard and it was capital letters hot in the middle of the summer for a Swedish boy. I recall only ducking into the gift shop, where my mind was broadened to celebrate air conditioning, my favorite discovery on my entire trip through America! Add to that Sprite, which came ice cold and went down my throat in a way no amount of expert advertising could have conditioned me to swallow. Another image from that gift store and visit to Tombstone, Arizona: My mother, equally exhausted from the heat, looking as if she was hanging onto the post card racks like a life preserver while my father continued his visions of gunfighters out in the graveyard.

What else did I discover? Wrigley's Juicy Fruit (I liked the yellow-wrapped gum best). I suppose our parents were giving us gum so we could entertain ourselves during the thousands of miles we traveled by car both summers. That's another thing I remember – my father bragging to others about the mileage he put on the rental car. I don't remember the exact number; it did not register, like so much else that was supposed to have during the mind broadening travel trip to America.

I discovered during our journey my love for motel swimming pools. After sitting in the car all day accumulating miles, what a gift it was to be set free in the pool and dive and swim and dive and swim. I also loved the kids-eat-free buffets, though I recall I was such a good eater that my very honest and straight-laced father was embarrassed and thought it was not right for me to eat free, so he paid for a "full" adult's buffet.

Another learning experience from the summer to and in America: We were in a place called Bryce Canyon and we were going to get to ride! Real, live animals! They were mules. I remember finding it interesting that these animals were a combination of horse and donkey. I found the way their ears looked different from those of a horse

to be a discovery. I also heard the head wrangler of mules and tourists tell those who were afraid and said they had never ridden before,
"Well then we'll give ya a horse that's never been ridden before!" My
father and others thought that was very funny. Years later, I thought
how corny this joke was and how often the wrangler must have said
it to tourists.

These are only a few, but the major memories of several weeks
worth of traveling in the U.S. when I was a boy from Sweden swept
across the ocean in an airplane by well-meaning parents. Did travel
broaden my mind? It did, as I discovered some things about human
behavior, all of it ancillary to what people might say when they ut-
ter the words "travel broadens the mind" or "travel is good for the
person." I am not sure I learned what my parents intended for me to
learn. Or did I? ❦

On Eggshells

Easter is upon us, and I say that with the feeling of affliction, as if I was coming down with *röda hund*. Well, not quite *röda hund*. When I was a child in Sweden I remember it was a painful disease and not as fun and common as mumps. Besides, mumps made nice cheeky egg shapes, which we associate with Easter, and appeared easier to get over.

I feel about Easter the way I feel about Christmas, conflicted and annoyed. If you really wish to know my thoughts about Christmas you would have to read a column I wrote for *Norsdstjernan*, which Ulf (that's Barslund Mårtensson not Nilson) luckily decided not to publish. Ulf, who is one of the most fair-minded people I know, said about the Christmas column, "We just can't run that," and in his voice was a sigh and concern not that he would be bombarded by angry letters, but that he simply didn't want to ruin Christmas for a lot of people.

So let me walk on eggshells, as we say here in America, as I feel compelled to write about Easter. By now you have had sufficient time to be warned so you can put the column away or use it to line a bird cage or the housing arrangements of some other small pet you might have. Which brings me to this "animal," a strange creature indeed. The Easter Bunny.

I don't understand why we have grown men dressing up in costumes that other people have sweated in profusely – though supposedly these for-rental outfits are cleaned between users – and walking around with baskets serving plastic or candy eggs to children. God forbid the kids should have to eat nutritious hardboiled eggs. Some parents even like to have their child immortalized in a photograph next to a big smelly costume of a bunny that looks like a relative of the commercial chocolate mix version with moth-balled, worn squirrel or other pelt people used to keep around their homes. These days, in the name of animal kindness, I am sure only synthetic animal skin can be found in homes and around people's necks. And in this kind of masquerading, wolf in sheep's clothing, lies the problem.

What in the world does a rental costumed Easter "bunny," with what could be a mass murderer inside, have to do with this holiday called Easter. Does Easter even mean Easter any more?

Those of you who have followed my columns know that I am not a formally religious person. I have been grappling with religion all my life. I have even grappled with it publicly in *Nordstjernan*, and as a result apparently stepped on Christian toes. But I had nothing to worry about, the mail that came certainly exchanged at least a toe for a toe. And some were very supportive, in what I think the Christian spirit means to be (no, not the Holy Ghost).

Growing up in Sweden and reading the Bible – both the children's Bible with illustrations that were very imprinting, and the less exciting (at least for a child) black-and-white book – I formed an image of Jesus riding into Jerusalem on a donkey. I don't have my children's Bible anymore, but I recall that my worry was the donkey. He (or she) looked so small compared to the bearded white man with slightly longish hair (not the long, long hair I encountered later). My overall impression from that encounter, and I swear to God I speak the truth: I was so worried about that little donkey and felt sorry for him or her, wondering how the little animal could carry the Jesus load.

By now I hear some of the Christian populace sharpening its pencils, ready to slay me with words edgier than Gabriel's sword, how dare I depict my experience with Jesus and Palm Sunday this way. But the experience I have described is exactly what bothers me so much about Easter being upon us, or, speaking for myself, Easter being upon me. I cannot for the life of me understand how we can celebrate a holiday that has been so adulterated, first with the giant Easter Bunny, then with the Giant Jesus on a small donkey.

Where I live in the Deep South, I have for some time seen beautiful, simple wooden crosses draped by purple cloth in people's yards. My three dachshunds and I walk past them daily, and no, my dogs are not tempted to pee on the crosses nor would I ever let them. You see, as I think about Easter, I, a person who is not very religious in a formal way, am overcome by the starkness, the purity of spirit, when I see those wooden crosses.

I then wonder what this world is coming to (no, I am not making any oblique references to the Second Coming), when in the Bible Belt celebrations that used to be called Easter Eggstravaganza have been renamed Spring Eggstravaganza. How has some kind of political correctness managed to usurp the original meaning of Easter? As a person who is not even formerly religious – yes, that is my mantra – I am saddened by this dilution of faith. I would much rather see people allowed to express their faith openly than resort to some kind of bland retreat. Where is David when we need him. Are Goliath/business and profits unassailable?

While we are at the altar of adulteration, I must share a flashback of my brother and me being *påskkärringar*. Yes, my little brother made a much more beautiful one than I did, and I am sure he would have won the pageant at *Blåkulla*. It seems to me the old custom is more pure and acceptable in that it represents a kind of intersection of paganism and Christianity, rather than lining up on store shelves chocolate or yellow-sweet chicks and aluminum-fatigued bunnies.

Or maybe I am just Scrooge?

Yours, smiling, I remain, your *skribent*. ♥

A Swede Appreciates Fourth of July

When I was a child visiting America, I remember
my aunt baking a deep chocolate layer cake
from square pans, and on it in the right colors,
the American flag was drawn in enough sweetness
to now make my teeth hurt. That was the summer,
too, she took me to a drive through bank,
and I recall getting from the teller a pen that had
a coin-shaped cap with the American flag on it.

It hardly gets any better than that for a child, no matter his or her nationality, and from what I understand now the summer of the Bicentennial that I spent under the tutelage of my Chicago relative was a big party, even by American standards.

This was the summer also of travel with the family out West, to behold the Grand Canyon, Death Valley, and a place called Tombstone that has set forever its mark in my memory that air conditioning was not a great nightmare, as I later read and understood metaphorically, in a book by Henry Miller. When you are a child, America is wonderful, whether you come from a developing country or the cool dark north of Europe, famous for its nonstop light if you catch it at the right time.

I establish my background as a U.S. citizen, as an American, which I became years later during a swearing in ceremony when I remember not being too happy about being corralled by my father to have my photo taken with my brother, fellow sworn-in citizen, under who happened to be president on that occasion, Ronald Reagan.

As an academic I am definitely conservative, two words which do not go together for most people when they think about the professoriate, no matter the recent showdown at Cantor Corral. But imagine a country where a young man can attend two schools in Texas, Trinity University and TCU, and get a great education and become an English professor. All the while going both with and against the grain, and no Dear Leader chopping my head off or someone banishing me to a cold place as if Solzhenitsyn's fate lived on for generations to experience.

Whenever I set pen to paper to write about America and Independence Day, or more accurately, begin to move my fingers across the keyboard, they assume a lighter dancing motion, a fluidity, that comes, so unlike a more stuttering and banging activity when I write about other subjects. I check my reasoning self to be sure I have not bought all the propaganda, but even so, how can one not enjoy some of the propaganda of America. Even Putin would be upset if we took away his privilege to travel to Disney World.

For all of its ups and downs and shows of extreme wastefulness, America is a country that has offered me so many choices in my life. This is not to say that if I had stayed in Sweden life would have been hell if we must also employ in our judgment that wonderful as it can be to some annoying American way of uttering and giving voice to things being black or white. But every time I begin to think about America I remember in my studies as an English major the Irish Nobel Prize recipient Seamus Heaney's lines of "The unquestionable houseboy's shoulders that could have been my own," of realities different, not peaceful, maybe violent and speech-guarded in other countries. Now I have choices, and yes, even Swedes celebrate Independence Day, have and do make the choice to call it that instead of 4th of July. ❦

Where Swedes Fear to Tread

I found it fascinating and horrifying to watch North Koreans cry in some sort of ecstatic, deluded state when their beloved Kim Jong Il died. They engaged in behavior that was as enthralled as it was thrilled, crying out of happiness and pain because they loved their leader so much. At least that is what the cameras on television let me see and had me believe.

Amusing, but also terrifying, has been the groveling behavior of military leaders and others of North Korea in the presence of the new North Korean kid on the block, Kim Jong Un, when like an idiot not trained in gun safety Un waved a pistol and any one of his followers appeared clueless that a random bullet by the finger of Korea's No. 1 chubby could easily have invaded their sparse bodily frames. They probably would have been honored to take a bullet from the man with the very un-Korean Chow-like hairstyle.

What I don't realize, apparently, is that for so many years North Koreans have been brainwashed and conditioned to know only one way, dictated by their government.

So I should probably give some Swedes a break; actually there a quite a few who live in some kind of politically correct, PC, world that has them engaging in the most selfish and at the same time self-destructive behavior, as well as in the destruction of fellow native Swedes, without knowing what they are doing.

I am learning this through keeping up with the Swedish press and also social media where misguided individuals let their PC-voice ring out, self righteous, at the expense of many a Swede who somehow has escaped the mass brainwashing that has occurred in Sweden for so long.

While fringe elements of *Sverigedemokraterna* are as much to blame as those of *Socialdemokraterna* in spreading unacceptable messages of hate, it is the Fifth Column – that has so much potential to do good – that is unfortunately engaged in mischief that is entering the territory of unconscionable acts.

The Swedish press by and large appears not only to be building the fire, but to stoke it, even pour gasoline on it. Furthermore, the Swedish press is engaged in schizophrenic behavior.

On one hand, the press is calling for everyone to get along in Sweden, but it loves to provide news coverage that escalates racial strife between native Swedes and people of other cultures or religions. One could say the Swedish press, in its coverage, is engaged in race-baiting and a kind of hate speech. Perhaps those in charge of the papers want to make money by covering news in a way that will have those Swedes who want Sweden to remain Swedish become angry, to hook these Swedes on divisive propaganda, the way Rush Limbaugh in the United States talks for hours on end to upset his already angry audience.

The problem with Swedish press coverage, compared to the rhetoric of Rush Limbaugh, is that the Swedish press speaks out of both sides of its mouth, and with a forked tongue.

It is as if the Swedish press gets up in the morning and thinks, "What foreign or why not Muslim thing can we cover today? And let's be sure it is something criminal, so native Swedes will get upset. Then, to hedge our bets, let's be sure to portray foreign perpetrators, who have done bad things, as victims. And, just to have all bases covered, anyone who wants to punish a criminal who is foreign – of a different race or religion – must be labeled a racist."

From the outside, the inconsistencies and contradictory elements are simply mindboggling.

For those of us who have lived in several countries and in the U.S., we have escaped the perpetual PC onslaught that Swedes in Sweden have been exposed to. We are able to see what the Swedish press is up to. But as Swedes we are also a good people and don't like to see in ourselves any sort of overly aggressive action toward others. We are, after all, neutral, whatever that means. But we have an obligation to speak up and help our Swedes in Sweden not only weather the storm but also overcome it.

As some of us Swedes living in the great melting pot of the U.S. observe, we realize full well and logically that Sweden must have a hard time – not only economically but also sociologically – absorbing the huge number of immigrants it has received. The politeness of Swedes in Sweden is rubbing out the native Swedes. Remember, there were clashes among natives and newcomers and different immigrant groups even in America during the years of mass immigration here. And yet, the United States is a country that was built by a mosaic of people of every religion, race and cultural background you could think of.

Swedes need to realize that every now and then it is high time to take a stand. A stand against the propaganda by the Swedish press; a stand against the self-righteous PC-Swedes who all too easily cause other polite Swedes to be silent or retreat, simply because the PC-Swedes, ironically, engage in ad hominem attacks, the cheapest and most illogical way to debate in a civil way. The PC-Swedes know full well that many honest, peace loving Swedes who are concerned with self preservation, including that of Sweden and the country, cower when they are called racist or xenophobic by PC-Swedes. Even the thought of being called racist or xenophobic by PC-Swedes will have many a good Swede sit by.

I am here not proposing that unless Swedes take action to prevent PC-Swedes from engaging in hate speech, all Swedes ten years from now will wear veils or Muslim garb; that prayer mats will be sold at IKEA; that *julskinka* will be forbidden. On the other hand, Swedes, do not let a minority of vocal PC-Swedes have their way with you.

Of course I am sure some PC-Swedes would have no complaints whatsoever if the Swedish culture and heritage were to become extinct. But that is a cheap shot to take, as would be suggesting that PC-Swedes take some charter flights to North Korea instead of the Canary Islands this winter and read online the hatemongering texts of Swedish media. ☙

Commendable Sweden!

Vladimir Putin, who resembles what one imagines could be a descendant of a bad part of the gene pool Swedish Vikings left behind when they practically founded and ruled Russia centuries ago, must be trying to exact some sort of warped revenge by irritating and antagonizing.

Sweden as Russian military operations have escalated over the past several months in the vicinity of Sweden.

The Swedish newspaper *Expressen* reported on October 11 that Russia has twice antagonized a Swedish research team for Sweden's Meteorological and Hydrological Institute (SMHI) aboard a Finnish vessel in international waters. Russian aircraft and a naval vessel were involved. The Russians forced Swedish scientists to change course east of the idyllic island of Gotland. The Swedes then reported sighting a Russian submarine.

This aggression by Russia appears to be part of a trend when one considers an uncomfortably close provocation by a Russian SU-27, coming as close as 10 meters to a Swedish Gulfstream aircraft. The incident occurred in international airspace over the Baltic Sea on July 17, and as reported by *Svenska Dagbladet*, this was one day before a Malaysian airliner was shot down over Russian-controlled Ukraine airspace. More significant, in voicing frustration with Russia's rogue behavior, *Svenska Dagbladet* observed that "these events should not be confused with those of Russian attack planes that violated Sweden at Öland on September 17 or the Russian bombers south of Skåne on Sunday, September 21."

Photos released by *Svenska Dagbladet* on October 2 show the Russian SU-27 heavily armed with missiles as it flies by the Swedish Gulfstream jet turning its belly for an in-your-face demonstration of Russia's power.

Then of course fresh on our minds is the latest installment of Russian aggression, the submarine saga unfolding in the Swedish press and reaching also the United States. The latest news, at the time of this writing, is that Russia has sent a military vessel equipped with a submarine hangar to presumably retrieve one of its submarines that has come too close for comfort for anyone living in Sweden – and certainly for the image-conscious empire-building Putin, who can do no wrong, as in having any sort of Russian military maneuver be unsuccessful or any of his "machinery of war" experience technical or human error.

These actions, under the watchful eye of Dictator Putin, should come as no surprise. As the saying goes, a leopard does not change its spots. Or, in the case of the no-longer youthful Putin, you cannot teach an old dog new tricks. We cannot expect from Putin any diplomatic skills nor any consensus-building capacity unless he does it his way, with sincere apologies to the great American Frank Sinatra. Putin, as a KGB man, is trained to spy, brutalize and act without a conscience, to carry out a mission like a cyborg.

From the actions of Russia against Sweden we can deduce that Putin must have his eye set on expanding beyond the Ukraine. How wonderful it would be for him to go sailing in skärgården (the archipelago) or bare-torso riding in Dalarna.

We are fortunate that the normally sedate and polite Swedes are standing up to Putin and not engaging in sissifying talk in foreign relations as practiced by the Obama administration. The courage Swedes are showing in a united front – the politicians, the military, the people – is commendable, especially considering the relatively small size of the country.

It appears the only true small thing in this entire matter, and paradoxically it looms large, is Putin's attempt to bully like a Napoleon wannabe, to try to create national pride, as if he could really achieve such by taking over Sweden in his dreams. The little man dreams of a land of real Vikings from Sweden, the way things used to be, a long time ago. And in a Sweden standing up against evil, Putin is discovering that in Sweden some things are still the way they used to be a long time ago: The Vikings are standing up to protect the homeland that is so dear to them. 🐦

Pippi Longstocking Censored, Swedes Next

Pippi Longstocking is being improved by Swedish Television (SVT) reported *Expressen* in an article with the headline of "SVT Removes Racism from Pippi Longstocking." In the 1969 version of the children's classic, Pippi referred to her seafaring father affectionately as "*negerkung*," which literally translates to "negro king," though the Swedish vernacular more or less means "king of the natives." This term and also Pippi's pulling on her eyes pretending to be Chinese is being reedited.

The children of Astrid Lindgren, the popular and prolific Swedish children's book author, who exercise tight control over the profitable Lindgren brand Saltkråkan, have approved the changes. They must have psychic powers because they maintain that their deceased mother would be all for these changes.

This latest revisionist maneuver by Swedish television represents yet another frightful show of political correctness and force. This summer Americans got a taste of Swedish Television's offerings on NBC primetime with the new Poehler sitcom series of *Welcome to Sweden*, originally produced for and shown on Sweden's TV4. As a Swedish-American I engaged in the unpleasant viewing experience of what was not a funny comedy and wrote several reviews of the show and show's episodes.

Perhaps it is funny in Sweden that the main character, played by Greg Poehler, who is the brother of Amy Poehler, who is also producing the show, appears ashamed and afraid of being an American so that when he encounters a character of Iraqi descent he begins a friendship in which he maintains he is Canadian and certainly not American.

The latest Pippi Longstocking debacle and appreciation for the Poehler *Welcome to Sweden* comedy by Swedes is part of a disturbing trend of the de-Swedification of Sweden. Like tall, proud timber Swedes have had a history of being cut down. After a long rule by the Social Democrats that included the disabling makeover of the country by Olof Palme, the country's ruling parties swung to the right, though in Sweden that would mean being to the left of the Kennedys and Nancy Pelosi, who no doubt would be flattered to be mentioned in Camelot company.

Swedish general elections were held on September 14, 2014, and while the Social Democrats will be able to maintain some power in a coalition government, the Sweden Democrats came in third. It should be explained here that the Sweden Democrats are a conservative party that has logically argued that Sweden cannot sustain mass immigration financially.

Unfortunately, the Sweden Democrats have been called racist and the Swedish people have been silenced or labeled racist if they even dared discuss the inability of Sweden to absorb a large immigrant population in need of immediate and substantial welfare, as they are entitled to by Swedish law. An editorial on Swedish elections in *The Guardian* should make it clear that even if Swedes want political freedom they will have to deal with propaganda such as this, from *The Guardian*'s view on the Swedish elections, 09.15.2014: "All of the action was on the right, where the xenophobic and reactionary Sweden Democrats more than doubled their share of the vote at the expense of the internationalist and technocratic Moderate party. The right wing that marches under a flag triumphed over the right wing that governs from its spreadsheets."

Any national pride of native Swedes continues to receive the harshest of criticisms and Swedish schools are giving in to have the meat their children eat butchered according to Islamic practices (according to daily *Sydsvenskan* of 04.24.2014, in line with Sweden's policy of non-religious schooling).

This butchery is a metaphor that serves well to illustrate what Swedes continue to encounter in their own country. But at least they appear to have a temporary stay of Islamic rule and the proposal of establishment of such a state within its borders, which cannot be said for its neighbor, Norway (all acccording to a report in the *Daily Caller* of 09.04.2014, which describes the threats by two Norwegian ISIS leaders). Swedes and Norwegians have long been rivals like the Texas Aggies and the University of Texas, but we can only hope that these two nations get together when both the famous bonfire and Bevo equivalent are threatened with extinction due to capitulation in what is a misguided understanding of what inclusiveness means. 🐂

My Waterloo with ABBA

The first time I became aware of the existence of ABBA my family and I, with friends, were glued to the television set watching the Eurovision Song Contest. At the time, our family had moved from Sweden to Austria, but we did a lot of traveling, so I can't say for certain if we watched this monumental event in Sweden or Switzerland, as ABBA drove through its competitors like a tank with the song "Waterloo."

I remember the event was cause for great celebration, not necessarily because the music was great but because Sweden had won. Our victory in that living room was as frenzied, tumultuous, on top of the world, as if we had just watched Sweden's national hockey team beat the Soviet Union.

In fairness to ABBA, as if ABBA needed fair treatment, I did find the rolling, driving force of the tempo of the song, along with the persistent, somewhat too-sweet repetition of "Waterloo" and "oh oh oh" to be interesting and memorable. I am sure I was not the only Swede or European to walk around with the tune stuck in my head for weeks on end. As a matter of fact, as I write this column, the music of ABBA visits me like a familiar guest. But like a guest, after only a short stay, it begins to stink like a fish, to rephrase very liberally an old Mediterranean saying.

I was about 12 when "Waterloo" first hit me, and other ABBA hits in rapid-fire succession invaded my pre-pubescent and then teenage years. "Money, money, money,... it's a rich man's world," I sing now from memory. The track switches in my head: "Take a chance on me..." Scary, a whole lexicon laid open, just like that.

I remember mostly key phrases from ABBA's songs, and that is no small feat for a group to be able to pull off. The only other group whose music I remember that way are the Beatles. I am not what you would call a musical man, and for me to have remembered anything from music is quite a feat to have accomplished, by the musicians. I do not know if the success of ABBA stems from the group's ability to create memorable jingles and catchy phrases. Perhaps. Because what really is the difference between "I do, I do, I do, I do..." and "Hamburger Helper, when you need a helping hand." Obviously, a glove and a piece of meat, and in the case of ABBA, two beautiful ladies as I remember them from my brother's sizeable double LP cover. No, Hamburger Helper jingles and "Money, money, money,... it's a rich man's world" should go down as some of western civilization's highlights.

Way back then, in a different century, I was humming and singing along to 33 ⅓ rotations of ABBA per minute, and even more often, ABBA ran through my head while I was walking or doing just about anything. Remember, those were the days before iPod, even Sony Walkman, barrages.

It was with some trepidation I recently turned to looking at ABBA lyrics. Trepidation not necessarily because of anticipatory avalanches of reader hate mail but because I did not want to find out if the text, or lyrics as musically educated people say, accompanying the catchy phrases and jingle moments would be cause for disappointment.

The "Money, Money, Money" lyrics were a big disappointment. All I learned is that it is a rich man's world, it would be great to live in it, the "I" of the song works all day and does not have enough money. Even plans to marry someone rich would fall through. Throw in a consideration of going to Las Vegas or Monaco to win and a not-so-original observation that "my life would never be the same," and we have nothing but a pastiche of clichés. Thank God the "Money, money, money" and "it's a rich man's world" refrain make a memorable jingle.

"I Do, I Do, I Do, I Do, I Do" (just how many dos are there?) offers nothing but cries of reassurance that a person loves another. The song would be meaningful beyond its jingle factor if maybe these polite protestations are really a battle in which the narrator is attempting to reassure herself that she really is capable of loving someone.

ABBA's "Voulez-Vous" sadly does not even a memorable jingle make. It employs the cheap device of using French to create a risqué title that would not have been permissible or sounded as good in English or Swedish.

"Nina, Pretty Ballerina" – I can hear the refrain coming from my brother's room – how nice a variation on the more troubled character of John Travolta who does a different kind of dancing in *Saturday Night Fever* just a few years down the road.

I kept on reading lyrics of the quite large catalog of ABBA and I was becoming, as I did not want to, disappointed. ABBA was and is good for memorable jingles but for a song to hold up overall, with interrelated imagery and sudden nuances – forget it.

On the other hand, to be fair – I did say does ABBA really need fairness – how much more artistic merit does the Rolling Stones' "(I Can't Get No) Satisfaction" hold. I am afraid the answer is a whole lot more. The lyrics, score, performance by the Stones is felt, whereas ABBA is all safe auto-pilot with a thick wax coating and travel in a safety-minded car, in comparison. Even the Beatles, with their tamer sound, evoke emotions that ABBA simply does not.

Perhaps the success off ABBA stems from its jingles you can't get out of your head, while the rest of the song, unfortunately, is filler.

But it is delightful to be Swedish and around the world to have it known that ABBA is the name of a Swedish group and not only seafood. But I sure liked those *fiskbullar* when I was a child. They were safe and soft to eat and delicious, not hard to digest at all. ❦

Finding the Middle Way

I can hear my wife sanding the kitchen walls as I sit and write at the other end of the house. A kitchen renovation project has been building inside her for at least six months, and fortunately my involvement is minimal.

I say minimal instead of non-existent because once in a blue moon I do step inside stores that sell things best not put into the hands of a man who loves to type. I am talking about saws, screwdrivers and drills – motorized or manual.

My infrequent visits to these stores, both the orange and blue one as well as the nearly extinct "mom and pop" operations, are a result of my very kind wife wanting me to at least have some input into how her, I mean, our home will change. On those occasions, she has already done the legwork, and usually I must only point to a tile or color swatch and the visit is over.

During those trips, however, I cannot resist going to certain aisles just to read the signs and names of products being offered in the name of home improvement. One of my favorite sections is the one that features poisons intended to kill insects, bugs and vermin.

It is not a favorite section because I am a killer or take pleasure in killing insects, bugs or vermin. I am not. I like the section because it offers me a chance to study language and its use, and along with it, cultural attitudes. The killing section, as I call that part of the store, has been one I've for years told my wife I will write a column about, especially when she asks, "What are you doing!?" with emphasis placed on the words indicating we did not come to the store to have me walk around indulging in vocabulary. Yes, she knows I am a bit strange, but must I really be so gruesome as to study that which involves roaches, bugs and the like.

So I will not write a column on American attitudes, product names, and ways the extermination of unwanted enemies is presented in the store of orange or blue. Instead, let me turn to the land of blue and yellow and observe how products that, shall we say, have to do with flies and mice, and their companions, are presented to their consumers.

You just heard me begin to adopt a more courteous or less aggressive attitude, and that is the case when it comes to killing pests in Sweden. This is not to say Swedes like rats and mice, or offer them cheese and send them to a governmental agency that has vast rat and mouse preserves where they roam free and happy. However, "enemy" is not a marketing strategy or attitude that concerns creatures and humankind as they interface in Sweden. Unwelcome or less-welcome house guests define the relationship between people and pests in Sweden.

Frankly, I was surprised that Swedes are allowed to kill pests, but they are. And everything is rather pleasant and polite, even cozy in this endeavor. In my research I found to my relief that pest-killing products are often endorsed or approved by what might be called the Swedish environmental protection agency and also by the Swedish board of agriculture. Both names, when said and heard in Swedish, along with their mission statements, also happen to evoke much friendlier reactions than their counterparts in the U.S.

So if you must kill pests in Sweden, rest assured that two nice governmental agencies can grant a kind of endorsement or even removal of guilt about the act you are committing. Should you have business to do with wasps, you will be reassured that you are conducting your business in an "environmentally friendly way." You will even be in for an educational experience as you "watch" how the wasps are drawn to the trap. Even better, you can buy this wasp trap in *"mysiga"* variations. (While it is difficult to provide an exact translation for *"mysiga,"* know that it can mean cozy; you can even check into a cozy/*mysig* bed and breakfast in Sweden. So I guess that is what the wasps are doing when you put them to bed.)

When it comes to mouse and rat traps, you can engage in the rustic and traditional. These are offered of course in plastic, but better yet, "classic mouse traps with wooden board" will fit in right to make things *"mysig"*. Be sure to also get the traditional *"flugsmälla"* (fly swatter).

The depiction of this tool made me feel right at home as a child on my grandmother's farm, where we swatted flies between eating pastries and lifting a glass of homemade *vinbärs saft*. However, for Swedes who have gone too soft to swat flies outright, they can make sure insects "die right after they have come into contact with the line" drawn by a "fly pen." The latter would be good for writers if they wish to demonstrate that the pen is mightier than the sword.

There was only one item in the ad I read as it relates to killing pests that made me squirm, made me feel that as a Swede I would be killing. But perhaps I am too sensitive. This product was rat poison, which was said to be "eaten by mice and rats without giving '*betesskräck.*'"

Either this term, loosely translated as "terror of bait," referred to the rodents being poisoned without being in agony or eating it without being afraid of it. Either way, this text brought to light that Swedish copywriters had not managed to completely make the act and process of guests leaving one's home sanitized, civilized or peaceful.

What did I learn from my journey into Swedish ad copywriting and mice and men? Obviously, I was not able to examine thousands of ads and devote a dissertation-length treatment to the subject. Based on what I found, I noticed, especially after walking the American aisles of ads and pest killing products, we have two extremes: the sanitized and friendly doing business with creatures we do not want in our house under the flag of blue and yellow and the aggressive, even proud killing of pests under the red, white and blue.

Isn't there a happy medium somewhere? Something, well, "*lagom.*" 🐀

Looking for a Church

I have not received a pledge card from my church. Apparently they are not looking for additional hymnals, new pews or maybe some tasteful decorations to facilitate worship.

I must say I am a bit disappointed that the Swedish Lutheran Church has not found me here in America. Surely my name must exist in a database somewhere, even if it is in scanned-in form because they had to go back to the days when I was "*skriven*" in the church by hand.

So nothing from my church. Not an invitation to come dressed to the parsonage as my favorite character out of the Bible. Jesus anyone? Or Cain or Abel, whichever one of those two brothers survived and got to eat the delicious soup. How about a postcard, "*Fika med Prästen*," especially if the minister is a she and hot.

No, I don't think my church is really into socialization the way American churches are, especially down here in the south. Jesus goes with everything here, from golf tournaments, to fireworks, to exotic cruise ship vacations, and I wouldn't be surprised if a church had not come up with a Christian-themed bake-and-decorate-a-cake contest.

When I was a sophomore in college, I took a summer school class called "Religion in America." I didn't take it because I am particularly religious; it just seemed like a pleasant way to earn elective credits toward my English degree. Visiting churches much of the time, to get out of having to sit in a classroom, what a deal! And the class was taught by an odd couple, as in Felix and Oscar: a very neat and uptight minister and a laid back sociology professor. The minister we called Dr. So and So and the sociologist by his first name, a simple two letter abbreviation.

During one of the classes, between visiting a priest who had no sense of humor and a church that was "progressive" – meaning it welcomed anything you could imagine along the sexual spectrum – I blurted out an answer to a question I no longer remember. "I was born in Sweden; therefore I am Lutheran."

Apparently this resonated with the sociology professor because from then on the class was fun, and I remember he gave me and one other student our final exam early, polishing in front of us with a clean kerchief two apples for us to eat.

Strange and not-so-strange how the human element and God mix with such great influences upon us, at least when it comes to the human part of the equation. Besides, I have never seen God. Have you? I certainly have not seen his son, Jesus. And quite frankly, I like life on this earth and don't really want to be around if the Second Coming should hit us all.

So Lutheran I was, and, I suppose, I am - compliments of being born in Sweden.

Did I have a religious upbringing? Not particularly. I remember being in church very few times. One of the best times was running around an empty church and playing hide-and-seek. Another time was some kind of festive occasion that my mother took me to. I don't think she took me to indoctrinate me but just so I could have the experience, much the way she took me to the zoo or the dentist.

I don't know how it came about, but when we lived in Lund I was part of some kind of youth group that was connected to the Lutheran Church. We spent time in a room that had extra chairs and tables - probably the folding kind - where we had to work on a craft project that consisted of cutting out felt animal shapes of different colors that had to be glued onto a burlap-type material. Something about Noah's ark, I remember. I also remember having some childhood disease which luckily got me out of completing this scissor-dexterity assignment. This in turn translated to a pastor coming to our house, blowing in like the wind and leaving us with the project he had finished. I remember my mother vocalizing to my father how energized the pastor was. She said it in an admiring way, without making him out to be special because he was doing "God's work" or something along those lines.

When we left Sweden and moved to Austria I became much more aware of religion. Austria, heavily Catholic, had ornate churches and all sorts of blessings by priests, including one instance of a priest actually bestowing grace upon a machine that was to operate in a factory.

Besides feeling surrounded by Catholics in Austria, I also felt cast out, the way I today hear people refer to someone as being Jewish.

My family and I were part of, for lack of a better term, the ruling class, but Lutherans we were. Walking on water could not have leveled the playing field for us.

Religious instruction was part of the curriculum. Lutherans and Catholics had to part ways during school when this subject was taught. I was deeply dismayed when a priest came into our classroom and yelled at the entire class, "*Evangelische raus!*" Even as a child I could see that the priest was taking pleasure in banishing the Protestants.

What would have happened if my family had stayed in Sweden? We certainly were not churchgoers. Would there have been opportunities for my "Lutheran development" or any sort of recruitment to the church?

The Swedes that I know are not a formally religious people and I have yet to speak to someone who would admit to or even pay lip service to making God part of everyday living. Whereas here in the south, "Have a blessed day," and "God does not want me to..." are uttered without so much as a raised eyebrow.

Swedes I have met are bland about their religion, if such a term is possible to assign with meaning. But surely this cannot be so for Swedes, when I read the uplifting columns of "*Präst i Kalifornien.*" Everything blossoms there. Perhaps she moved to America because she could find more of a fertile ground for faith here. But those are answers only she can provide.

Meanwhile, when I knock on Swedish churches in my mind, as imagined in movies and books, I find no one home or only someone who is mentally deranged or fanatic. Surely these are artistic reactions in an existential world and not the reality of Swedish Lutheran churches.

I await your answer – whoever, wherever you are. ☕

Distressed Furniture

I remember, unfortunately, the day my eyes first caught the horrific sight of distressed furniture. At the time I did not know that I was looking at "distressed" furniture.

My wife, who has impeccable tastes and superhuman talents when it comes to decorating a home – and that's hands on, accompanied by sweat, back- and tendon pain she never complains about – had brought home a new piece of furniture. My wife asked me to come into our guestroom, where all newly acquired home furnishings are quarantined, to look at the new piece. For the record, unless I am really in the mood, I have about as much interest in looking at newly acquired household objects as at baby pictures, or worse, babies in-person that often wind up making unpleasant sounds.

The new piece of furniture immediately made an unpleasant sound that went through the entire core of my being, including the financial jugular. Whatever the "it" before me was – a small night stand with doors below a table surface? – I immediately saw a crack on the piece of furniture my wife had just adopted.

I bent down, with some difficulty, frame of 6'6" and the aging process being co-conspirators, and, yes, as sure as my back felt uncomfortable, there was an unsightly crack running a few inches across the wood. There were also tiny unsightly holes all over, as if some insect had held a drilling party.

"Is this used furniture?" I said. In hindsight, my voice must have been accusatory. It is not that I consider myself too good to own used furniture but I have for a few years now been grateful that my wife and I were able to pay off our student loans and so are able to treat ourselves to first-hand furniture.

My wife, who knows me very well, took no offense but began to educate me on "distressed furniture". In return, I offered a lecture on why would anyone spend hard-earned money, or even found money, on something that looks as if it has been beaten, neglected, bumped, even urinated on by generations of large pets.

And the term "distressed." Surely the marketers could have chosen a better name. Our society, by its own admission and proof of sales pitches of commercials, is constantly combating stress. In a society where even a scratch on a car causes the psyche of many a person irreparable pain and things need to be sleek or glossy, evenly matte or grained, is there really room for what is surely worse than stress – DISTRESSED – especially if one has to pay good money for that bad look or state of being?

Youth and youthful skin and bodies are a commodity, and emulation and aspiration to achieve such are a major best-seller. And people want to spend big money on distressed furniture? Apparently so. I have seen in America beautiful youthful models sit among things distressed. How depressing it would be, or maybe not, to behold instead old and wrinkly people lounging in a living room featuring beautiful, new, shiny, polished tables, chairs, cabinets, and whatever else my limited vocabulary in the realm of furniture cannot name.

Let me blame the appeal of distressed furniture on America being a relatively young country, and maybe there is a large segment of the population with a psychological bent for old-looking things. This would mean a yearning for the past, insert your own psycho-jargon here.

But I remember the old days, "the good old days," and also have heard about the good old days. Good Swedes would take care of their possessions and maintain them in the best possible condition. Is a good Swede now someone who aspires to fill a house with furniture that if it were human would have hoards of workers from social services descend upon the scene of crime? Has distressed-furniture mania spread across the sea to the homeland?

To find out, I contacted some Swedes that have not left the old country. One, Carl-Gustav from Skåne, showed a dry and wry sense of humor (how Swedish!) while providing facts and opinion. Some of the humor would be lost in translation, so I produce the original in Swedish below.

"Vad jag vet har inte detta fenomen
[distressed furniture] nått Sverige ännu. Vi
brukar ju ligga efter er. Jag skall höra med

bekanta om någon känner till det. Skall till Stockholm i nästa vecka. Kanske har det kommit dit. Det påminner mig om trasiga jeans som säljs för dyra pengar i affärerna, vilket jag aldrig har kunnat fatta. Återkommer till dig om det har nått Sverige."

I was relieved that at least one source confirmed my belief that Swedes still take pride in appearance and keeping things neat. Even if Carl-Gustav brought up that he could not fathom why some Swedes would buy ratty jeans and pay high prices to dress themselves this way. Oh well, there are always outliers, even in a country that has been known for its homogenous people and culture. But I just had to be sure Sweden had not been invaded by banged- and scratched-up furniture.

I decided I would approach the oracle for what is branded Swedish furniture, in Sweden and across the globe, the arbiter of tastes for so many consumers. I emailed IKEA. I had never emailed IKEA before, not even to complain about their assembly instructions that are all in pictures featuring a unisex or sexless creature that make furniture assembly frustrating.

While it has become fashionable and also a badge of honor among many to complain about how long it takes to assemble IKEA furniture and how awful their instructions are, when it comes to responding to consumer inquiries, IKEA deserves an A+. Ylva Magnusson wrote me two emails, in the course of 48 hours, despite the fact that I had emailed when the workday for Swedes would be over.

I learned that "distressed furniture" is called "shabby chic" in Sweden and some Swedes like this kind of furniture. But more important, at least in my own mind, I was relieved to learn that many Swedes like a "country style", something which is a really clean retro look. As far as Swedes embracing furniture with holes and cuts that don't serve a functional purpose, whew – Sweden the old country and Sweden the new did not disappoint. Swedes have not fallen for distressed furniture so many otherwise rational and intelligent Americans pull into their homes as if to assemble a junk yard for all to display in a house that is worth several hundred thousand dollars.

In the interest of fair disclosure, even though this is an opinion column, IKEA does have some products, according to Ylva Magnusson, so that "you can in a DYI way give the products the look of old and used yourself." IKEA also has an interesting blog that shows what Swedes like in the ways of furniture.

And what about that piece of "furniture" that my wife brought into our home? Either my vision is declining or my wife has established harmony by humoring this Swede who apparently is not as American as he thinks he is. When I tiptoed one night past the guestroom so as not to wake our smallest dog who yaps (endearingly?) at the slightest movement, my eyes saw the piece of furniture. Its wooden cabinet doors were smooth, and they had a pleasing color. There was even the faintest smell of new paint in the air. As I moved in closer on the object, the piece still looked new.

I rubbed my eyes. No, sleep and allergies were not deceiving me. Good clean lines and smooth surfaces a Swede can be proud of are the way in our home. Besides, in another ten years our non-distressed furnishings may be in vogue again. And if by that time shabby chic furniture has taken over Sweden, well, as the saying goes, we'll cross that bridge when we come to it. I only hope there is a troll to take care of matters, should they get out of hand. ♥

Lund: Of Pocket Knives and Flashlights

When my family moved from Stora Harrie to Lund, I am sure an initiation of sorts occurred for my brother and me. Not that Lund was a great cosmopolitan area with skyscrapers, but certainly some would say it had more to offer than Stora Harrie.

I do not remember any initiations involving "country bumpkin meets sophistication." If there was sophistication in Lund, I at no time felt accosted by it. The initiation I remember involved flashlights and pocket knives. That's right, I associate Lund with flashlights and pocket knives. May Lund's bureau of tourism rejoice at this association!

Male initiation rites of yesteryear, when viewed through modern eyes, even those trying to explain them in sociological or anthropological terms, appear a bit ridiculous and not relevant to what our current society needs or tolerates. So even in the late 1960s in Sweden, killing a lion with a spear, to prove my manhood at the age of 7, was out of the question. Besides, *djurvänner* (PETA) and the local police would not have looked favorably upon such an activity. And my family would have had some explaining to do if we had hauled in my 6-year-old brother after having circumcised him on the narrow balcony of our row house. Slaying a dragon or other great enemy was also out of the question, no matter how much under the influence of *Röde Orm* or Tolkien's scholarly fantasyscape from across the water.

So what male initiations existed that would be tremendously exciting and allowable and not bring the wrath upon my family in the form of Wallander characters descending with horrible Ystad dialects upon our newly built Lund dwellings?

Pocket knives and flashlights, flashlights and pocket knives.

The ritual of a father giving his son a pocket knife seems to have all but disappeared. However, I still have mine, found in a drawer of desk accessories, where it sleeps in an elegant leather etui. Out of its case, Swedish steel and a royal coat of arms greet me. I am still cognizant of my father being proud of the fact that the knife was Swedish steel. I also see his hands pull out the blade from the very thin knife, his voice proud to tell my brother and me that it was very sharp and we must be careful.

He also showed us the file the pocket knife contained. Less enthusiasm there, both from him and me. I did not find it useful when I tried to use it as a kind of super sandpaper on wood. No doubt the file is meant for a "gentleman's manicure." My father's eyes had a special gleam when he showed the bottle opener that was among the three functions of the knife. I loved the sense of adulthood, the kind of territory of forbiddance I had now entered at the age of 7, being able to open bottles of beer.

I don't remember my brother or me actually using our knives very much. Sure, we tried to undress the occasional piece of wood, and I remember the greenness and sap I encountered in doing so, but that act was never as valuable as the understanding, the unspoken gift from our father's eyes as he bestowed upon us each our very own Swedish steel pocket knife.

The other tokens of Viking totemic qualities in a modern era were the special flashlights my brother and I each received, identical like the knives were. My father showed us how to use these flashlights, experiencing with us a kind of fascination of the possibilities that handheld and battery-powered instruments of light held.

At my current age, I am able to discern the fascination my father shared with his sons: What more than a flashlight and knife would a boy need to explore and conquer the world? An entire civilization could be built with these tools, propelled by the spirit of the Viking. If centuries ago these men could sail and row their way to continents as yet unseen, what possibilities might there be for my father's boys given these basic tools to stimulate our explorative imaginations?

I wish I had the flashlight in my possession still. Years ago, when I came across it during one of my many moves, I was taken aback for a moment by how cheap, yes cheap, the construction of the flashlight was. Yet to my brother and me it appeared sturdy and as exotic as a balloon to take us on a Jules Verne journey, even if the guy was French. No doubt the flashlight appeared sturdy because it was heavy in our small hands, the metal foil filled with "D" batteries.

The things it could do and where it could take us, this flashlight, in our darkened bedroom! By pushing a switch forward we could produce either a green or red light. By pressing a button we could blink and blink. Blink blink blink! And the games of chase we played on the walls and ceiling. My red spot catches yours, or my green spot never keeps pace with yours, but that does not matter. I don't think we ever used the "regular" yellow light, preferring to ensconce the little bulb inside with a red or green plastic "shade". Of course part of the magic was that we did not know how the red or green light was achieved, other than by the push of a switch. Our cognitive abilities did not play catch-up for a while, and we did not care to find out what was behind the magic. That would have been a distraction from our adventure in Lund that traversed all time and space when we were the handlers of the lamps.

I doubt very much any Swedish boy today would feel a sense of initiation when given a flashlight or pocket knife by his father. And I am not foolish enough to say we should go back to a time when things were simpler, as if we could. But how stimulating or how meaningful are initiation rites today? Do they exist? Are Swedes or children of any nationality observing stages that encourage a sense of maturity, and with that maturity possibilities powered by imagination and a sense of exploration? Or is it all one continuum of merely observing and then buying the next edition of the iPhone? What would the Vikings have done? What should the Vikings of today do?

Somewhere a ship is sailing, or it has sailed. ☙

Showers
in Freedom

When I was a child I remember being shocked when a friend's mother told me they were not allowed to take a shower after a certain hour at night. My friend lived in something called a *lägenhet*, a word that immediately took on an ominous meaning in my mind. I thought it must be frightening to live in a place where you weren't allowed to get clean when you wanted to. Of course at that age I did not realize people in high-rise apartments lived so close together with walls so thin that such washing rules might help light sleepers get a good night's sleep.

Imagine asking or telling Americans to take a shower only during certain hours or to sign up in advance to do laundry. I realize now, as a transplant to America, how lucky I was to grow up in Stora Harrie, Sweden. Compared to where my friend lived like a cooped-up chicken in his *lägenhet*, my life was more of a free-roaming and even organic chicken in Stora Harrie.

We lived in a yellow brick house with large front, back and side yards. Trees separated us from one neighbor, the other neighbor was a farm field. Where our backyard ended, a huge grass field began. This was open range for my brother and me to play in, although our yard was large enough that I do not recall feeling the need to venture beyond it, despite being a very curious little boy.

During part of the year, my mother's *solblommor* (sunflowers) appeared to grow overnight into the tallest creatures I had ever known. I thought of these flowers not as part of the flora but felt them to be, albeit eerie, persons. They stood tall against the wall of the house that faced our one neighbor, unseen through vegetation.

Then one day they were mysteriously gone. I do not recall ever seeing my mother cut them down; they simply disappeared. The memory of them appearing is actually more prominent in my mind.

We had thick, tall trees in our backyard, and I remember learning how to use a hammer and nails without supervision. It was great, innocent fun to hammer nails into the trees. It was hellish when my *mormor*, who lived very nearby on the farm, and from whom, unbeknownst to me, my parents rented the house for a very reasonable fee, dropped by unannounced to pounce on me and my little brother like some female version of Thor. It is the only time I ever saw my sweet and generous grandmother become unhinged. She was angry, chastising us and my mother, and went from tree to tree, pulling out each nail.

Other adventurous memories, compliments of living in Stora Harrie rather than a frightful *lägenhet*, came in the fall. My father, who had a vast wingspan and the lungs and heart of an Olympic swimmer, erected just outside our yard a pile of leaves my brother and I could have taken diving lessons in. As if the magic of watching leaves assemble into something so big so quickly wasn't enough, my father applied gasoline to the leaves and a fire blazed in the sky, smoke following. I am sure if I had looked on as a teenager I would have imagined my father with his pitchfork standing by as a kind of grim reaper worthy of an appearance in a Bergman film. But that was the beauty of living in Stora Harrie at a young age: I saw nothing of lasting terror, collecting instead impression upon impression of adventure after adventure.

One such adventure happened when I opened the door to the cellar in our hallway. Steep stairs led down into the dark, cold, uncharted territory as far as I was concerned. In my child's myopia I did not see several cabbage heads that for some reason my mother or father had left on the top stair. I nudged the cabbages and they began to polter down the stairs. All I remember is my father going berserk, thinking about how the cabbage would be damaged or there would be a mess for him to clean up.

More sedate memories include receiving a fresh beet that the nice lady next door had dug up. She even told me how to prepare it. And in the winter, deep with snow and ice, we'd wait for a tow truck to pull my father's car out of the garage which was at the bottom of a curving slope, unpaved and steep. How fun to watch the truck like some benign giant move my father's car that appeared toy-like. Nothing like winters in Stora Harrie, with snow and ice that lasted!

I stated earlier that I did not often traverse beyond the boundaries of our yard, but I remember one occasion when I did. I wanted to visit my grandmother, who lived on the farm nearby. Many times we had driven to see her. We simply took a right out of the steep bowels of our garage, drove past a field, hung a right, and then drove down a rather long and unpaved road that made great clouds of dust in the summer.

I must have been reading about something that had to do with expeditions. Perhaps my mother had opened the world of Nils Holgersson for me. The rare telephone call was made to my grandmother, and I set off to visit her, with anticipation of a reception of all things sweet to eat and drink. I knew the road by heart. But instead of walking along the road, I decided to take a shortcut across the field. To this day I don't know how the idea occurred to me that I would save time and effort by taking a shortcut, but I had the impulse and followed it.

I remember the outcome of that journey well. To me, the plowed field had always looked very orderly; I had observed the furrows and what I thought were only slight differences in the height of the soil. What I came to experience and remember was that my ankles hurt badly as I trod across what tractor and plow had made – along with a lack of rain – into something very solid. When I arrived at my grandmother's farmhouse, I was weak and exhausted, and my ankles hurt as if I had been out skating on a frozen pond for hours.

Today I think about my friend in his *lägenhet*, both parents working, all of them home. He and his parents must be quiet in their two rooms. Quiet not only because it is getting late and no one is allowed to take a bath, but quiet because his parents are tired, and as much as they would like to, they cannot let him out to play several floors below.

Of course I don't know if my friend in his *lägenhet* was really suffering. But I also don't know how much of a difference it might have made if he had been fortunate to live in Stora Harrie, land of the fields, poltering cellar cabbage, jumping in leaves and guarded by the sunflowers that stood over a childhood that passed soon enough. ☛

Print of Peace

A print has traveled with me through the years.
A trained eye – even an untrained eye, provided
the person was an adult in the 1970s – will notice
the frame as a popular one from that decade.
And a kind of matte glass protects the print.

For as long as I have owned the print I have been aware of the frame and glass as much as of the contents. It features what art critics and lovers would call a naïf scene depicting Sami in a winter landscape, some of them in sleds drawn by reindeer, a background of tents, against a backdrop of too many reindeer to count. A kind of steep white mountain, presumably covered by snow, holds up one end of this world. A few Sami are walking between the tents. The entire scene is done in crayon, mostly black, with some orange and blue. There may be other color graduations, but if that is the case, I do not notice them when I look at the drawing, either in my mind's eye or from a rather short distance.

I say rather short distance because there are times I will stop and behold the scene when I enter our laundry room, where the print hangs centered above washer and dryer.

Some might think hanging the picture in such a space is disrespectful or outright foolish, considering a laundry room must have some humidity that cannot be good for art. Well I have always thought art should be enjoyed without worrying about investment value, so the naïf reindeer scene continues to hang above generations of washers and dryers. It continues to live, and no one can say it is being damaged by sunlight where it hangs during all sorts of rinse, spin, and various dryer cycles.

I inherited the print from my father. This in itself makes it of special value to me, which is not necessarily true of things just because one inherits them. My father always had a special love for the print and so did I. It was not a love inspired or instilled by him, but we must both have some primitive component in us that admires what I am sure Jung would find to be a depiction of the collective unconscious.

So there is my Jung hanging above what increasingly is quieter and using less water.

But the print's value, as far as I can discern, stems from its reappearance in my mind over the years. When it happens unannounced, I find peace and solace are the results. I cannot explain why reindeer and Sami and a Nordic landscape are so comforting. I just know these elements are.

In more recent years I have noticed the year the print was done. In large numbers next to the name of the artist is written "1943." That is the date I am drawn to when I see the print across the width of the washer and dryer. My eye is drawn to the year and signature of the artist after I have taken in what is such a peaceful scene. The year begins to ask me questions, such as where was this artist when World War II was raging and how much did World War II influence this artist? And: How strange to produce something so calm and just that during the Second World War. Or maybe not.

I do not know who the artist is. I was fortunate to receive the print before the Internet was readily available to destroy investigations and speculations that took effort, to be replaced by instant information that comes now at a heavy cost and with flat or no feeling. Ironically, it is a "flat" so different from the term used to describe a work of art drawn without three-dimensional perspective. I have been tempted a few times to Google the name or the letters I can make out to be the artist's name, along with the year and "World War II." But I am still not sure I want to Google anything about the print or artist – even after I have now written about my experience with it over the years. What will the Internet really tell me? It is much like going online to "learn" about the horrid school shooting that took place in Connecticut. Without wanting to avoid the subject, I don't want a media experience from my computer. I have a feeling that I went to look at the print of the Sami and their reindeer in a snowscape this afternoon because somehow what I know of this killing tragedy has affected me enough to cause me to seek comfort in what was drawn in crayon by an adult who made art in the hand of a child.

I know that when I go into the laundry room again, this time to retrieve the leashes of our three mini dachshunds for their nightly walk, my eyes will want to fixate on the number "1943".

I will not let them. ❧

Stubborn and "så jävla envisa"

Swedes are stubborn and self righteous, and I should add the phrase *"så jävla envisa"* to that observation. That's the thought I had when I was checking my voice mail to see if my mother really had a left a message. You see, for a few months now, my mother insists that she leaves voice mails and I insist that I can see she has called but there is no message from her.

There are plenty of voice mails from other people, however – from all over the United States, even regions I would think have no cell coverage. And my mother lives in a region that is as cell-covered as it is traffic congested. And that can best be described as immensely.

But this will not turn into one of those sad columns about grownup children and their elderly parents in one stage or another of dementia – and I certainly hope that day never comes – though the stubborn Swede in me thinks I'm right about my mother having something wrong with her phone, and for an instant thought she has at least become forgetful or doesn't know how to use a cell phone. This same stubborn Swede knows the other stubborn Swede, *Mamma*, is thinking her son is considering she might have Alzheimer's or does not know how to work a phone.

So we are now a few months into the war of the cell phones, the son calling the mother to talk to her and she telling him she has left messages and he should listen to them so she does not have to repeat what she already said and so they can spend valuable synchronous phone time discussing her messages or other topics.

Unfortunately those other topics in synchronous conversations – yes, we still manage to meet on the cell phone with regularity – are taken up by suggestions from the mother that her son get a new cell phone, and the son not giving in.

Just this past week I received two messages from her. One was, "Have you gotten your new phone yet?" The other: "I am calling from outside my house to help you pick up this signal."

So the messages have gotten through. But I am not aware that Mom has gotten a new cell phone. And I certainly have not. So where lies the problem or the solution to this mystery of dropped phone calls? And let's not even drag my brother into this, who also has not received numerous messages.

Of course he and I keep in touch by email, "trash-talking" in the little text window on Words with Friends, the occasional cell phone call when either of us picks up, but the feud of dueling cell phones between the eldest son and *Mamma* is here to stay for a while, I think.

Which brings me to more amusing stubbornness involving communication in the family. Of course *Mamma* is involved. She refuses to use a computer or any technological device that would transmit data other than voice. But she does have a fax machine. What she does with this fax machine is the following: She writes notes and letters by hand and faxes them. But in order to receive them you have to have a fax machine. But the ink for the fax machine is expensive, especially when all sorts of things are sent that have large black areas, or even drawings. Mamma is very creative. Fortunately, while I have a fax machine, I can only use it to send by plugging it in manually so as not to disturb our land line that we are not dedicating to fax.

So the war of the cell phone, fax and landline is alive and well among two stubborn Swedes: Mamma and me. While I am not giving in, the other day I went to purchase 36 FOREVER first class stamps, printed out an equal number of mailing labels which I affixed along with the stamps to number 10 envelopes, and now I am going to send my mother all sorts of little thoughts using my favorite ink pen.

This action on my part does not mean, however, that I am acknowledging my mother is right. I await my mother's commentary about these thought-missives through the mail, something with her sense of humor, "I hope you didn't buy too many envelopes with too many stamps. What if I die before you can use them?!" Then that Swedish "*Ja,*" from her - a kind of sigh and chuckle in the same breath. I love my stubborn, stubborn *mamma!* ♥

Of Mom and Monkeys

When my mother was a little girl on a farm in the south of Sweden, she wished for a monkey. She even believed someone would bring her one.

As strange as this wish might sound in today's regulated pet industry or as normal as it could be in a world where money supersedes laws and makes many a wish come true, apparently my mother's desire remains unfulfilled to this day.

I don't know if it was her seafaring uncle who put the thought of a monkey in my mother's head. He did bring her bananas and they might have been the natural connection to a strange furry animal from an exotic locale. He was a captain and a scary man – even years later when I saw him in the sitting room of my grandmother's large Swedish farm. Whatever "grog" was, my mother's uncle would have lots of it on those visits. And who knows, after a few drinks in the late 1940s or 1950s, the captain might have proclaimed loudly to his niece, "A monkey you shall have!"

For a long time I did not know my mother had wanted a monkey so badly – the subject never came up when I was a boy. It must have been a secret like a childhood wound.

It wasn't until I became a long distance runner and frequent-flyer consumer of bananas – four a day – that my mother confided in me. This happened in my late teens, when my mother had been loaded down like a pack mule at the grocery store to feed two teenage sons. With 16 bananas or so, she had been asked by the cashier, "Do you have a monkey at home?"

My mother must have felt compelled to tell her teenager, who wanted to go live in Africa to study the chimpanzees like Jane Goodall, of her longings for a monkey. At the time I lectured her on the difference between apes and monkeys, clearly not ready for the two person dialogue.

Over the years my mother sent me clippings of chimpanzees, usually engaged in some activity I have little patience for because I find anthropomorphizing to be demeaning to animals, even if it is the human that is the fool. In defense of my mother, chimps really aren't too far removed from us homo sapiens doing the same stuff.

But it was still a one-way feast, my mother sending me ape- and monkey-related items in the mail.

As it relates to my mother and me, it was last Christmas that my understanding of dialogue requiring two people was mysteriously summoned out of my DNA or behaviorist skin. And it was commercialism, like a sea captain bringing bananas from a port far, far away, that set things into motion.

While home for lunch and sifting through a stack of catalogs with mailing labels bearing my wife's name, I found a catalog with my name on it. There, on the bottom of the right-hand page over which I was chewing my cheese sandwich: a remote-controlled monkey! This was it, a gift ready to be sent to my mother, as all the forces of nature and mischief in me came together.

What mother in her seventies would not have use for a monkey that walked and talked? Even the batteries were included, so I would not have to hear the complaint of "you did not send me any batteries."

I love the beauty of shopping online – no wrapping, no packing anything, just give a complete stranger your credit card number and an instant thought becomes another's reality within two to eight days, depending on how much you want to spend on shipping.

I went to the catalog's website and clicked, typed in numbers, clicked again, and could not wait the two days until my mother would have on her doorstep a thousand miles away a remote-controlled monkey!

A week went by. Silence like a megaphone. Another week, silence translated into daily thoughts of why hasn't she called? I have given her the monkey she desired all these years. And surely she would not have been happy if I had arranged for a live chimp to be delivered to her immaculate house. I gave her the remote-controlled monkey, one that doesn't shit all over her white carpet, and I want some feedback, damn it! But had I given my mother any feedback all these years when envelopes with monkey- or ape-related matter arrived in my mailbox? Of course not.

Two-and-a-half weeks, and my mother and I spoke on the phone.

"Did you like the monkey?"

"Well, your niece played with it."

"Did she like it?"

"No." And in my honest mother's voice I could also hear that she did not care for the remote-controlled monkey I had sent her.

Is there a lesson to be learned from all this? I think the answer is clear, and I know it, each time I look at the little plastic monkey bobbing his head as he sits on a plastic leaf, his movements compliments of solar power on the back porch.

He came about two weeks after my mother and I had the remote-controlled monkey conversation.

I like this monkey and have told my mother so. She has not told me if she donated the remote-controlled monkey, but I am sure there is a little girl or boy somewhere who, at the right age, is enjoying a monkey before it is too late. Does anyone have any gift ideas for my mother? ☛

IKEA and the Great Chocolate Heist

Swedes are known to be a peaceful people, contrary to propaganda such as that found in a book sold at Disney World intended for children. The book began with the question of "Who Were the Vikings" and immediately provided the following answer: "People who lived in Scandinavia (Sweden, Norway and Denmark) over a thousand years ago. They were fierce warriors and seafarers who attacked towns and villages all over Europe. The Vikings were hated and feared by their victims, which isn't at all surprising."

Just imagine a book being sold about people with black skin and rendering them this way. But this is not an article about double-standards when it comes to race and what passes for acceptable coverage in the news or media. Perhaps the book sold at Disney World had it right if by extension we accept that Swedes today have some Viking blood and characteristics.

What is it then that has Swedes up in arms and has turned on the nasty protestation part of their make-up?

Ironically, it appears IKEA – a company so inherently and supposedly associated with Swedes and Swedish-ness and all that is good and kind and peaceful about the people and the race – is waking Swedes up from their slumber in comfortable IKEA decoration land. I cannot resist here including news from the Swedish newspaper *Expressen* this week, which features an article on a Swede having made a porn film featuring IKEA products, including their catalog, with the title, "I F. . . . .G LOVE IKEA." Along these lines, less graphic but on a more aphrodisiacal note, this one involving the mouth and tongue, Swedes living in the U.S. and across the world are fed up with having IKEA brand chocolate bars shoved down their throat.

Swedes are demanding, and rightly so. So much that Ingvar Kamprad peers out of his retirement cocoon and grants the working masses with money to spend on Marabou chocolate for purchase, which some say IKEA, with impure or profiteering motives, has taken away like candy from a baby in the IKEA food market store. Swedes have been left holding the bag, empty or filled with inferior IKEA brand chocolate.

The gravity of the situation is such that several social media sites show wordy showers of aggressive demands that Marabou be restored to shelves at IKEA, these coming from the stereotypically taciturn Swede en masse. When *Nordstjernan* on its Facebook page recently posted something about Marabou, a barrage of "missing Marabou" reports ensued, a Bring Marabou Chocolate to IKEA and grocery stores Facebook community page was begun, and all the while the Facebook page Bring REAL food back to IKEA SwedeShop continues its noble quest for real Swedish food products such as Marabou chocolate. Perform a Google search for IKEA chocolate and you will find representations involving the product and human anal section, more mischievous photo montages of IKEA chocolate involving a mother punishing her child and Putin not looking too pleased having IKEA chocolate bar imprinted in his forehead. Meanwhile, the fantasy of being able to purchase Marabou at IKEA continues.

What is the answer? An IKEA Chocolate (AKA Boston Tea) Party, where Swedes practice civil disobedience and empty the shelves of IKEA store chocolate skipping the register barriers or walking backwards against the arrow in IKEA stores to throw out the nasty IKEA chocolate? Is this the answer to what IKEA has pulled off, the great Marabou Chocolate Robbery, rivaling Briggs's great train robbery, only directing it at everyman and everywoman who knows his or her chocolate?

IKEA might save some of its image if it issued a public statement along these lines: "At IKEA, we believe our customers must eat IKEA chocolate. What we sell is what they eat." If IKEA were upfront, admittedly this in-your-face statement would not be the beginning of a great love affair, customers might respect the Swedish blunt honesty, instead of having to wonder if IKEA is involved in some devious plot to withhold Marabou chocolate from its loyal customers because IKEA is planning more corporate profiteering.

As the producer of the new porn film, "I F. . . . .G LOVE IKEA" stated, we do have mostly a positive relationship with IKEA furniture. Perhaps what is now a love-hate relationship caused by IKEA's Marabou interruptus could be mitigated by a re-introduction of the pure milk chocolate Swedes and citizens of the globe have come to know as Marabou and love like an old friend.

While the spokesperson from IKEA, when asked about the new "IKEA movie," did not have much positive to say, maybe this time IKEA will send out a corporate messenger to give us the good news: "Let customers eat Marabou Chocolate. Ingvar wants to do one last good deed, and he says to reward longtime IKEA customers with Marabou. After all, IKEA believes in more than a one-night stand." Or does it? ☛

Welcome to Sweden

In order for something to be funny – in Sweden
or the United States – it must first be funny.
The challenge with being funny is that being
deliberately funny is not very funny.

No, I am not talking about the entire episode of the new NBC show *Welcome to Sweden*. I am referring to the opening scene in which a celebrity, played by Amy Poehler, cans her accountant, played by Greg Poehler (that's Amy's brother in real life, whatever that is).

While the accountant is trying to tell his celebrity client that he will have to drop her because he is moving to Sweden, we see Amy Poehler "act," busy with the smartphone, texting away, so that, make no mistake about it, we can see that she is self-absorbed. This could be a funny moment, but these days we are so used to self-phone obsession (not a misprint), that the character better do something really funny or gross with the phone to gain our appreciation. Yes, Amy Poehler is phoning in her performance.

If you want more gross or attention-getting action that will evoke laughs, especially from an American, Puritanical audience, the sauna scene in which Poehler (sorry and thank you, no Amy) is about to pass out on the lower level of the benches to which his intolerance for heat has delegated him, delivers. Watching Poehler react to the father of his girlfriend, played in an impeccably modulated performance by Claes Månsson, who stands before him naked and gives him a hearty (perhaps this word is misplaced) welcome to Sweden and the family is must-see TV. Unfortunately the scene is marred by NBC's huge square pixilation of the father's butt, but we can still manage to concentrate on the expressions of the jet-lagged, alcohol-fatigued Poehler, whose face is just about within reach of Pappa Birger's schlong.

While we are on the topic of bodily functions, the scene in which the entire new family is celebrating the Swedish tradition of crayfish fest is funny as it is dominated by the loud sucking of crayfish heads by Swedes while poor Poehler is trying to explain why he has come to Sweden.

In this scene and in others, it is the mother of the girlfriend, played by none other than the beautiful-as-ever Lena Olin, who is truly funny. I don't know if her comedy translates well in the captions (I immediately and automatically switched over to Swedish), but she is hilarious in her matter-of-fact, yet outspoken ways about many things. Even though the song and protestations about Randy Newman's hit "Short People" has run its course in America, Olin adds a whole new dimension to being obsessed with people who are short. In both verbal and physical comedy she is one to watch, to watch twice.

The new-found family on the island during the beautiful summer in Sweden in a red summer house includes the brother Gustav of Poehler's girlfriend, a kind of loser, a Swedish Cheech and Chong of clear alcohol, a specimen that shows there are indeed Swedes that have physiques measuring up to Chris Farley's, may this great comedian rest in peace. He has nothing to worry about from Christopher Wagelin, however, who probably just needs more practice to bring a piece of humanity to the two-dimensional portrayal so we will be more amused by the stock character he has to play.

If there is someone who steals the show or at least holds his own, it is the American-crazed, movie-obsessed Bengt, played by Per Svensson, who owns a video store and comes across as a deliberate version of a kind of Dennis Hopper renegade, only he drives a red Mustang. Svensson's performance is an example of how a stereotype can be turned into funny when an actor has talent. That's right, he does not phone in his performance.

I have not yet said anything about the girlfriend, Emma, played by Josephine Bornebusch, who is beautiful with teeth so white and hair so blonde that she lights up the Swedish summer night where there is perpetual light. Her Swedish accent in English is barely noticeable and when she smiles it is refreshing to see a bite that has not been corrected by an orthodontist. She is touchable, real beauty, and it is understandable that Poehler has come across the giant pond to "find himself" in her company.

I have not yet commented much on Poehler's performance, all the while marking the review with his name, instead of that of the accountant he plays. That is because Poehler is the pivot around which the comedy revolves, this carousel of sometime merriment success, as he is like a breath of fresh air, excuse the cliché, and the perfect foil for other characters to react against. When I first saw him appear, I thought he looked like Greg Kinnear. This guy, Greg Kinnear also, has talent and it is marvelous to watch. Poehler is Everyman, if there ever was a likeable Everyman, and I hope there still are. I could see Jimmy Stewart take Poehler under his wing, in a time warp.

What was less marvelous to watch, besides strange pixilation, including a moment the movie-crazed Bengt said something, was an awkward cut to commercial during the crayfish celebration, followed by a quick flashback afterwards to the mutual "firing" scene between the Poehler siblings.

There also appeared to be two kinds of movie, yes I am aware this is a half-hour comedy TV show, playing, one with horny, happy, romantic Poehler and girlfriend in the car, and the closing of the episode when they sit on the dock and kiss and proclaim love in the midsummer night light. And in between, sandwiched, American-style, using two pieces of bread, is the comedic artillery. There was simply too much crammed into one episode, I hope is the explanation.

What did I think of *Welcome to Sweden*? There is that wonderful Swedish saying, *lagom är bäst*. That would have been good advice for the show to take. Don't try so hard at times. But maybe things will find a way to work themselves out in the long run, if the show has one. ❦

The Dangerous Kitchen

The kitchen is a dangerous place. While it might look idyllic as portrayed by Carl Larsson, I have found it to be more a place where the urban myth of "did you hear about some guy who microwaved his cat, and it exploded" is tame compared to at least nine injuries I have sustained over the years.

Lest this be construed and constructed as a sexist piece, making the Swedish or Swedish-American male into an inept domestic bumbling idiot, some women no doubt have encountered the dangers of which I speak. They, too, have survived while navigating this part of the house they pay such attention to on television shows that obsessively offer tips on how to spend money on renovation. If it were up to me, a kitchen would be an annex the size of what realtors list as a half bathroom.

But back to the theme of "Danger, Will Robinson!" – the saying that entered American culture in the 1960s with *Lost in Space* and has infiltrated my international mind.

I have given the danger and first source of my pain a name: dishwasher. How many times I have bent over to empty this labor-saving device only to injure my back, even when just approaching the top rack to take out mugs and glasses that also annoyingly drip water on my hands or hold a little pool on the bottoms of the turned-upside-down containers, during an act that offers also the moral quandary of "to dry or not to dry" with a towel before putting the dishes in the cupboard.

My back even went out before deciding to take the shortcut of not wiping the upside down mugs and glasses! So this labor-saving device – the dishwasher invented in its early form by a woman named Josephine Cochrane who was annoyed by her domestic help doing hard, manual work on her china – cost me $4000 when I needed an epidural after laboring to transport just one mug out of this dishwasher. Thank you, oh foremother Josephine, for my punishment and pain. And really, if we must put on our feminist caps, as a male I well deserve to feel pain requiring an epidural, lazy that I am in the kitchen.

The Swedish word for dishwasher, "*diskmaskin*," is so much more appropriate, as it holds it its provenance the danger, the evil of the machine that awaits the unsuspecting man (or woman) who comes near.

My kitchen, which by the way has idyllic Carl Larsson prints framed on its walls lulling one into unsuspecting comfort, has been like an ocean with sharks prowling. One of the sharks is a kind of pan that looks very modern and has a gliding surface to which nothing sticks. When I enter to do my biannual cooking - scrambling eggs (the other would be to boil water for pasta) - I touch the handle of the pan to pour the paltry fruit of my labors onto a plate, and I scream in physical pain worthy of the mental pain of Munch's famous painting. The soft salve of the buttery eggs offers little in the way of healing. I will wear a bandage to work the next day. Kitchen men of the world, cry "unite!"

I have also known sadness near the place I have little use for when my wife cuts onions. But let me offer us all some advice: Do not complain about tears from onions or any other smell coming from the kitchen if you are not the one doing the preparing or cooking. And while cutting at the kitchen island or counter, be sure to have clean towels on hand to stop your bleeding when you try to cut, for example, a tomato. When your blood flows, you might hear, "Why didn't you use a sharp knife," and you will be able to add to your disappointment that the tomatoes somehow look as if they were sliced in the wrong direction. My tomatoes never look like the ones I see other people present for sandwiches.

Once you have stopped your bleeding after the encounter with the kitchen knife shark (and learned you should not use the good kitchen towels to do so), get ready to use costly bandages (have you checked the prices of these things lately?) and experience the inconvenience of typing while wearing these highly touted products (read the descriptions on a Band-Aid box sometime, or stay tuned for a column on this topic).

I also do not recommend hand-washing any kitchen utensils while you are wearing bandages because they will fall off or take on a texture you will not like, despite the manufacturer's claims of being water-resistant. Be careful when you enter the sudsy water, hands like flesh submarines. Of course you can burn yourself (getting the right temperature of the dishwater is not as easy as you would think), but worse is the inevitable discovery of a knife shark in the water. Time for more kitchen towels and Band-Aids.

So there you are with several fingers compromised, back hurting, standing in your Carl Larsson graphic paradise of pain and danger, no longer able to enjoy the prospect of one of the summering Larsson family members being pinched by a crayfish, because you know pain is no longer idyllic. You have become a living performance art project, and you want to banish all and everything related to the labor of kitchens to a Viking's dark hall of never neverland.

You decide you will leave this world behind, sit down and relax in your Adirondack chair on the porch, outside, away from the inferno of whatever kitchen would be called in Latin or Italian, and you pour some left over coffee into a mug, open the microwave (no exploded cat innards in yours to clean up!), put the liquid of salvation into the center of the spinning wheel, shut the door, set the timer, and what the #&@*!, stars and pings, pings and stars – you rush to shut off the microwave.

What do you know. Your mug had some tiny metallic decoration on it. Well-read (with reading glasses) that you are, you know metals and microwaves are a no-no. But reading glasses to use a mug in the kitchen? Sufficient optical assistance or not, you don't need a ping pong game going on in the microwave. That could signify real "Danger, Will Robinson!" with results as depressing as the fates of the victims and "happy" characters of a "Wallander" episode starring Krister Henriksson.

But you are happy, at least as happy as someone in Wallander Land, that no one else is in the house to witness yet another expert move in that dangerous place called a kitchen that really should be a half bathroom or converted into a permanent takeout food strategy.

You take the coffee mug and thank your lucky stars nothing bad has happened to the microwave or you, but you are paranoid that some kind of chemical reaction might have occurred that would not make the coffee good for you, so you pour it out in the sink, carefully checking that no knives are sticking up from it like stakes in an animal trap in a political animal documentary. You throw away the mug just to be safe, and then you check your coffee maker. Out of luck, no coffee left.

Very carefully you walk to your car. God it hurts to sit down, your back just can't take this, but somehow you manage to steer with one or two remaining fingers to the local Starbucks. You find the drive-thru to be unoccupied, get your tall Sumatra and drive off, savoring the thought of sitting outside in your beautiful backyard, sipping coffee and listening to birds sing and squirrels chatter – now that your fingers cannot move across the iPad very well, you must instead listen and watch – and as you turn the corner to head into traffic, "AAAAAAHHHHH!" Why does it hurt so much when hot coffee makes contact with your thigh?

Carl Larsson, take me home. There is Skåne roast at the bottom of the shelf, and I ask my wife very nicely if she will make me a cup of coffee. In return, I will tell her of my adventure in the kitchen. I will be brave.

No, I will imagine a world where wooden butter knives are my oars, the *osthyvel* the most dangerous object known to humankind. ☙

"From my Mobile Office"

I frequently get emails with a signature line that reads, "Sent from my mobile office," or some variation thereof. Of course my problem is that I start thinking about this one line more than the content of the email itself.

I envision a small wooden house, a version of an old fashioned Gypsy wagon, with wheels punctuating the ground to make the office mobile. Then I have really devilish thoughts and imagine how crowded it must be inside this office, the smart phone, from which the message is sent.

But the question is: Why do people have to declare this? I immediately want to resort to Bartleby's "I would prefer not to," as I am taken back to the days when firms had rows and rows of scriveners participating in the annals of business. They wore high collars, like those you've probably seen from one of the period pieces broadcast by Masterpiece Theatre. Sitting in an office, touching wooden desks, staining fingers with ink, the dip of the nib of the pen signaling the start of the workday, the first movement up and out and across paper, and the final moment of the nib landing to perch in its holder, the clock with gears calling for all business people to end their day.

I am not in the business of sentimentalizing how office work was done in those old days, when certainly no one had ergonomic furniture. By all means, recline comfortably in your turbo Volvo seat with lumbar support and text business communiques from your mobile office. And you are even allowed to talk in this future we inhabit – at the very least to Siri (iPhone's voice-controlled personal assistant) if you are stuck in freeway traffic along with other business workers in mobile offices.

But there is no ending the work day now. The workhouse of Dickens' times now lives like a haunted building we inhabit forever, even if it yields good to very excellent pay. We may be able to stop our Volvo to play golf on a Friday afternoon and send something from the links via our "mobile office," but work now does not stop for us. Yes, this is a kind of twisted variation on Emily Dickinson's famous lines, "Because I could not stop for Death / He kindly stopped for me."

We are facing an eternity of work, in a world of leisure that people of earlier centuries could not have imagined. But is there really any kind of massage, fly fishing vacation, opera, even Abba song that will take the kink out of the "Sent from my mobile office" signature line and erect us from our stooping reality, as we emerge from the wagon of the minstrels in Bergman's *The Seventh Seal* and remember the half-admonition of "You with your visions and dreams." ☙

Good vs. Evil Was Once Clear. Or Was It?

If you could look onto our back porch around lunchtime, you might see me sitting back in a chair that is wide and deep, with great cushions. You will also see me holding a Winchester rifle with lever action. If you look closer, you will see it is a John Wayne commemorative rifle.

Am I an overzealous protector of my wife's flowers waiting to shoot squirrels with a caliber rifle that would send the squirrel leaping into the sky or splash the plastic windows of our birdseed feeder that serves as a snack machine for our squirrels throughout the day?

No. You will see me cradle the gun, the way you have seen John Wayne or any other movie cowboys, protecting fellow travelers or settlers, many of whom are family members. Only my .32-40 Winchester carbine with a saddle ring is not loaded. And I take strong sips of Sumatra coffee out of my mug during this grownup timeout at lunch. You see, I have a love for the old west, fictitious or real.

I love especially the movies from the 1950s and the early episodes of *Gunsmoke*. They are depictions and testimonials of good vs. evil, where those two elements were clearly defined. When the bad guys happened upon settlers, it was clear their intentions were to harm good, innocent people and it was equally clear that the cowboy hero, and sometimes a pioneer woman, would use a gun to protect the lives of the innocent. The innocent could then go on with established order and peace and enjoy all those little things that were a big deal in the westerns, such as Joey drinking a soda pop or Janey catching a fish off the banks of a clean creek. When Marshal Matt Dillon shot someone, it was to protect the lives of the innocent. And he, too, took no pleasure in killing. In fact, in one episode when he had to shoot an evil man he expressed his condolences to the wife of the man.

I am by no means condoning the act of killing another human being. What I wish to convey is that weapons can protect us and those we love when the stakes are either kill or be killed. At present, guns are the only way for those of us who are peaceful to continue to live and preserve our way of life. This might sound like a strange notion for some, considering these words come from someone who carried a Swedish passport until he was naturalized a U.S. citizen in the late 1980s. This same person kept a distance from weapons and hunting, great passions of his father and younger brother. I should just come out and use the first person singular, but as you can see, even now, when it comes to the issue of guns, I somehow slip into a distancing third person narrative.

I remember hearing of and tuning out exploits of my father who hunted moose in Sweden. I looked at wildlife covers of some kind of Swedish hunting magazine and never opened it because I knew it related to animals and killing. When my brother and father returned from the hunt, I noticed a scent that did not please me as I caught a whiff of them, my nose in a book. Today I know it was sweat mixed with gunpowder that invaded my nostrils and non-approving consciousness.

How do I know this? From Sherlock Holmes-like deductions of an adult who ponders the slightest thing and impressions during every waking minute? No. I know this because this afternoon I returned from a firing range. The scent still lives in my shirt.

Do I like the scent? Not particularly. Do I feel manly and bloodthirsty? Heavens no! Did I go out to the firing range with a nefarious purpose cloaked in the back of my mind? God no!

I went to the firing range to shoot my Smith & Wesson Model 29, 6 1/2" barrel, blued, .44 magnum (the gun made famous by Clint Eastwood as Dirty Harry) because I live in a small city that has become increasingly violent. Peace-loving people are gunned down frequently for money to buy drugs or even toys. What is a lover of peace to do? Call 911 when faced with an intruder high on drugs inside my family's home? Sic the three mini dachshunds on one, two or three intruders? Start a dialogue about violence, the socio-economic and mental health realities of America? Not at that time. You see, I want my family to continue to be able to live. I want to be able to spend time with my nieces. My wife wants to be able to continue her volunteer work. I want to be able to play Words with Friends, both when I score above 100 in one move or lay out letters worth eight points, the latter score bringing joy to my brother. Sound selfish? That I want to live to be able to experience the little joys and the big moments that life has to offer?

So when you see me cradling my John Wayne Winchester rifle and sipping a mug of coffee at lunch, be happy for me, because this is a time I can think back to the old west as I imagine it. Should you happen to come by my garage where I am cleaning my Dirty Harry revolver, trying not to inhale the fumes of the oil and cleaner, stop by and we'll chat about what your children did today, or what you hope to do with them when you go on vacation. You see, I am just a person who wants to continue that strange journey we call life. And you might be a person like that, too.

Unfortunately, I have to bear arms, that overused phrase, not to overthrow my government or rob my neighbor, but to maximize the odds that I will be able to stand there cleaning my gun and trying not to inhale the bad vapors so that you can come around and we can have a pleasant chat. And is it not Swedish to want to have a pleasant chat about the weather, and let's not forget the need for another mug of coffee... ☛

Summer Dream

I am in a dream, a very pleasant one. I see green foliage everywhere, through the windows of the car where I am sitting in the back seat, speeding by the Swedish summer-scape. In front of me, like mannequins, my uncle drives his "*kaffekokare*" (as my father refers to Carl-Gustav's noisy Saab), and to the right, where I can see his profile, sits my father.

It is strange that we three are traveling together, since my father is usually in some foreign country and travels mostly by airplane. My uncle Carl-Gustav usually drives a tractor across vast fields. But summer has brought us together, and I am filled with anticipation – both the good and bad kind – because I have entered uncertain territory. My father and uncle are taking me fishing for the first time in my life.

We stop at a cabin-like structure that is a store, it turns out. My uncle is strangely generous and buys me a Mars bar, not the chocolate of its U.S. namesake, I will learn years later. In hindsight, the name Mars is most appropriate, because I have never seen my father move his green bag with fishing gear from the hall closet, and Uncle Carl-Gustav has not shown any irritation toward children (me) all day.

I learn later that my father needed *röd-sprit* for his Abu smoker, which the store had, and we stop also to buy me a fishing rod with reel. I realize this is a big deal, both because it costs money in a household where money is tight, and because I am now to not necessarily gain my father's approval by learning to fish, but more importantly, not gain his disapproval. Of course as a child I do not know all of this explicitly, but a child like a dog can intuit, sometimes better than adults who have lost or suppressed their instincts.

This is one of the first times in my life that I have traveled on a road that is not pavement: We turn off the black asphalt onto a forest path and take a bumpy way that causes my uncle to speak adult language toward a parking lot that we know is a parking lot because logs have been placed like markers for automobiles to rest near.

We get out, and like the seven dwarves (although we are only three), march toward a little toll house where my tight uncle uncharacteristically pays admittance for us. A few more steps and we enter a narrow passage that my father explains to me is a rock quarry. What I really see are huge gray boulders and dark water everywhere within the circle of stacked rock. A little path, like embroidery, surrounds this lake.

At a place somehow determined by the adults to be the right one, with my father telling me to be quiet, we put down our equipment and I see my uncle and father get out their fishing gear. My father uncharacteristically comes close to me and assembles my Abu rod and snaps in place the reel, which he tells me absolutely not to lose because it is expensive. The preparations made, I watch the two men cast out, standing there with my pole, assuming my time will come.

It is not easy to be young and barely able to tie one's shoe laces and then cast out and reel in with varying speed, with a mission to catch a fish. But somehow I manage a few casts, some of which meet my father's approval. He, meanwhile, has caught two fish, and he brags that he is catching them on equipment that is old and costs a tiny fraction of what the man across the lake has spent on his fancy fishing gear. My uncle is fish-less, and I think this amuses my father.

I feel a tug. I don't know what it is as I have never experienced this feeling before, and I begin to get excited, afraid and filled with hope. I reel in. My father notices and starts to shout out instructions as if he were directing me to tackle another kid while playing soccer.

I am now certain it is a fish – I have seen its fin-flapping body out of the water – and my father's shouts drown out any sensations other than I better land this fish or I will be chum bait.

I feel my father's arms around my shoulders and his hands on mine, and together we are reeling in the fish. I smell my father, the scent similar to when he returns from hunting. He tells me to hold the fish, don't let go, and he leaves me for a moment to get a catcher, and it is both anti-climactic and exciting when the fish is caught between the eyes of the green mesh.

I notice my uncle is not particularly excited, but then why should he be. He is fish-less and a bachelor who does not understand children. And I am sure my father will tease him mercilessly if he does not catch a fish and I have.

My father is hyped up the way I have seen him only at ice hockey matches, and it is all because I have caught a fish. It is a strange journey I am on, and it is frightening and reassuring to be away from my books and silence, where I can hear only my thoughts, knowing my father is somewhere on an airplane, or maybe as close as a postcard that arrives from the Golden Gate Bridge in San Francisco, where he tells me one day we will drive together in a big, air-conditioned car.

For now I am in his hands, with fish, and we will return, after smoking the catch in the saw dust sprit metal container, in Uncle Carl Gustav's *kaffekokare* of a Saab. The sun sets and goes up over the grownup when he is a little boy. ☙

The Language That Just Won't Stay Buried

I mourn the disappearance, yes, the burial of "my language," Swedish, the way I mourn dead loved ones. I compartmentalize. As best as I can. File away all sights, sounds, smells, whatever constitutes memory. Don't leave a document visible on the desktop, let it be hidden under a document name I do not even associate with the memory and leave it in a folder not obviously labeled.

Clearly there are problems that come with this strategy, as the mind like a computer with powerful RAM can and does instantly retrieve associations. When I see a tulip, for example, I think of my father, knowing how he loved tulips. When I speak with my mother on the phone and hear certain words in Swedish, a whole world of words opens up that I thought I had successfully buried.

But I should know better. If ancient civilizations can be discovered and uncovered, my few decades of a past in which I spoke, heard, read and wrote Swedish on a daily basis, is easy and ripe for the picking or plucking.

There are certain words in Swedish that when translated never have the sound, sense, meaning, or impact they hold in a language my father was trying to keep alive during our move to Austria and then the United States by buying Swedish books for leisure reading, ordering required school texts and an *ordlista* as if my brother and I were Swedish students. But even his best intentions became extinguished by the need and want of young males wanting to fit in with the norm of their newly adopted countries. The goal for some reason, at least for me, was to pass as a native speaker of the particular country in which I resided, and to do that, I felt I had to turn off the background "noise" of and everything that went with being Swedish.

Even my well-meaning parents were complicit in this transformation, chameleonic, changing colors like the flags of each nation. And who can fault them for changing, as they too were exposed to new cultures and languages, leaving *gamla svenskan* at an unfair disadvantage in a competition. My parents continued to speak Swedish, but the added languages of German and English ended in "Swenglish," as my mother referred to what we spoke at home. This "Swenglish" was then pitted in almost sparring fashion against American English - parents vs. their children. It is surprising that Björn and Ulf as teenagers in this battle did not name themselves Bear and Wolf.

I don't want to give the impression that my brother and I became John Smith or John Wayne - we did carry with us some of our Swedish culture - but it was not a driving force in our lives. We had become Americans in that famous melting pot, but in our case it should be referred to as smelting pot, considering how eager and active we were in our pursuit of fitting in.

But the language of Swedish lay just beneath the surface of that new veneer of all things American, and unfortunately it was not used for a long time. And when it was used later, it was for professional reasons, such as business communications, translation of literature, a kind of cold, detached, fleshless experience. It was as if language and cultural background had divorced themselves without my brother and I knowing it was happening. We had become like tourists when we dealt with things Swedish, language or culture. Well-traveled tourists, but tourists we were.

And this brings me back to language, my Swedish that I mourn like a dead loved one. This person was someone I knew very well, loved, felt every nuance of existence of. But that person is dead. Even though I now have come to terms with this death and am facing it, I am encountering a greater sense of loss because I have missed out on the changes of the language, English imports into it, even slang, a professional and chronological growth I will never be able to recoup.

I don't know that there are any answers for Swedish-Americans who wish to avoid the losses I have just described. Making time to watch Swedish television, read Swedish books, speak Swedish, continue to eat Swedish foods and observe at least some of the traditional holiday occasions - these are good approaches but still will leave some of us mourning. And if we want a more optimistic ending to this experience, we can say, "Now we can't have it all, can we?" Depending on how Swedish we are we will or will not strike the last sentence. ☙

Why I Love Torturing My Students With William Faulkner

We will get there. To this point. And if you have read William Faulkner you know that a sentence of his can reach a page and sometimes that is a very admirable artistic creation, and often his long sentences are not necessarily artful. But the man did receive the Nobel Prize, and it was the Swedes that gave it to him in 1950, having awarded him the Prize in 1949.

The Swedes had been after him for quite some time, even translating and publishing an early short story of his, "A Rose for Emily," now famous and anthologized across the globe. The story brought Faulkner some very much needed cash – the man was always in need of money – when in 1930 it blew into the living rooms of Americans, and likely their minds, too. And what strange reading it must have been in 1932 for readers of *Bonniers Litterära Magasin* to read the story "*En ros åt Emily*," translated by Artur Lundkvist. The story has often been strange enough for Americans to this day, so what would Swedes have made of Faulkner's rendering of the American south?

But the human mind and spirit, even soul, are remarkable when it comes to cultural learning, both through study and also immersion in another culture. If someone had told me years ago that I would like Faulkner, I would have told that person he or she was *inte klok i huvudet*. If that person had told me I would be living in the Deep South and actually able to relate to William Faulkner's world, my actions might have been unconscionable. And teaching William Faulkner. But read on and decide for yourself about cross-cultural boundaries.

My wife hates Faulkner. With a passion. So when we got married, there was no problem with my raiding her book collection and appropriating the novelist's *Light in August*. I still have the copy, its blue-and-white cover, inside my wife's signature in a girl's handwriting, and a few notes made in the margin, mostly dutiful markings of what must have been "important" passages according to her professor at the private liberal arts, Catholic university where my wife majored in art history.

Some might think what strange reading for such a school and at such a young age, freshman-level, to learn of the castration of the character Joe Christmas, initials J.C., a fact not lost on critics nor, I would think, an involved administration at an excellent, liberal arts college with a small student population.

I teach Faulkner at a public, state college several times the size of that tiny parish of sophisticated learning my wife called home before transferring to "keep it weird Austin," and about half of my students are black, the other half white. Many of the students do not come from a background where academic preparation was a priority, given, or demanded. Many of them would have little in common with my wife if I cranked up the time machine and traveled back 32 years to put my wife in my classroom, where students every year read Faulkner's "A Rose for Emily" and "Barn Burning."

I have yet to come across a student who expresses hate or dislike for either story, and it is not because I am a Faulkner "nerd," aficionado (though that term would seem to fit the readers of Hemingway more), proselytizer, or other noun of distinctive "let's celebrate Faulkner" classification. In fact, I tell my students, like a kind uncle, with a loving smile, how my wife hated Faulkner when she first had to read him and that she is happy that I have such passion for Faulkner. Yes, this all sounds as if some psychological dynamic worthy of a Faulkner work, and God knows Faulkner has been worked over every way, to the extent that the man should now lie completely flattened out in his grave, from all the steam-rolling by his higher education disciples throughout the years.

But my students, for the most part, really like, even love Faulkner. And as I tell them, in a kind of cleaned-up version of I'm your uncle Anthony Bourdain, we will carefully read Faulkner's texts and provide textual evidence in our dialogue in search for motifs and

meanings, and I am going to continue to torture them and generations of students to come with reading Faulkner.

Why is it that my students enjoy the torture of Faulkner so? Semester in, semester out, in advanced composition courses, the inevitable modern American lit survey, narrative techniques, chronological confusion, even that notorious assertion that Homer Barron in "A
Rose for Emily" is gay. Apparently students have learned this in high
school, through some "undercurrent" of criticism or had a "daring"
teacher who mentioned this one facet of the story.

While I am not a firm believer that Homer Barron is gay, I find this
facet to be an asset in students reading Faulkner. I tell them from the
beginning, in passing, I know you will want to tell me that Homer is
gay, and I get a conspiratorial look from my students, as if they are
suddenly more awake and in tune to learning about literature than
their Red Bull has made them.

Herein lies perhaps the secret why I am able to continue to torture
students with reading Faulkner and they find this torture to be much
less so than did my wife, even I experienced it, also at an exclusive liberal arts undergraduate institution. Students are ready to talk about
issues and realities today that my generation were either not ready
to talk about or did not know about when we sat in school benches,
seemingly the only and strange, remaining common denominator
we have with today's students.

The readiness could be of course a product also of my students' being from the Deep South, right to the left of Florida, most of them
having lived their entire short lives in an unsophisticated city they
wish to escape, where only minutes outside indiscernible boundaries cotton and peanuts make up the economy, along with what is
strangely not promoted by a chamber of commerce that will pro-
mote the smallest thing, the large fact that Martin Luther King Jr.
was jailed in Albany, Georgia.

Students want to talk about the black characters in Faulkner's
two stories, but not in any sensational way about the term Faulkner
employs, nor in any complacent way, as might be expected from the
term's wider usage today. It is the socio-economic aspect students,
unprompted, seize upon in "Barn Burning," where they recognize
economic injustice rather than as priority the "evil" of the barn-burn-
ing, white sharecropper Abner. They have turned upside down for
me the value system with which I came to the story. For all the talk

about looking at things from all sides – something we academics say as automatically as we brush our teeth in the morning – my economic background had not taught me to approach the story from poor vs. wealthy. And the issue of race – written about by critics, the vast majority of them white – has much more meaning for my students in the classroom and me, than articles that assign all sorts of metaphorical "blackness," even a "white diaspora," the results of more "enlightened" and recent Faulkner criticism. I am sitting in a classroom with students many would call "rednecks" and blacks, who are close still to an agrarian life, not because they are necessarily farmers, but because they have family who has practiced this profession and many of them continue be in the economic underclass and can relate to Faulkner's "southern-ness," even a story such as "A Rose for Emily," first published in 1932, which means 82 years ago, a number eighteen-year-olds have no chronological feeling for whatsoever.

And for all the talk about the nuclear family being in prime non-existence, my students "get" the family values that Abner is trying to instill by "mentoring" his son Sarty. What you and I might consider child abuse, students find to be a family trying to stick together, without the judgment even the most liberal among us would find to be unacceptable. As one young woman volunteered, her boyfriend lived in a neighborhood where doing the right thing would not be to warn Major de Spain, this act would be considered snitching.

And what about all the "murder and mayhem" in Faulkner's "A Rose for Emily." Students, brought up on a huge diet of television programming that now also includes vampires, zombies, and just about every variety of crime show, welcome the mystery aspect of this short story as generations of students before were not trained to do. Students respond to the more sensationalistic aspects of Faulkner's nature, where "Southern Gothic" is cool, to use my generation's word for approval.

I could, as a Faulkner aficionado (sorry, Hemingway) go on and on about the students enthusiastically being "tortured" by my repeated tours through Faulkner-land, but as the old saying goes, space does not permit me to do so. What the current time does permit me to experience, however, is a joy of teaching that would not have been possible when it comes to William Faulkner's work even ten years ago. The planets just seem to be aligning themselves for students to be able to have in Faulkner an entry point into literature, into material many of us, and generations of students we taught, did not, could not find. But I will not be greedy and count on this phase or wave to continue for a long time.

For now, like Sarty, I will just enjoy the maturation process of this appreciation of Faulkner's work, both by my students and me, in a communion that exists in the land of Twitter and other technological prodigalities so many are fond of mentioning as if proof of students' short attention spans and inability to relate to the "old days." And I would like to hear from Swedes who have experienced William Faulkner in Swedish and not necessarily experienced the American South firsthand. ☙

My Beef with 50+ Commercials

My wife and I are watchers of news programs on television at what we like to think are youthful ages of 50 and 51, respectively. Though yes, the arrival of AARP membership cards and the magazine and bulletin have taken some adjusting to which no reading prescription will ever fix. And it is difficult to ignore that this AARP is a membership leading into death. I feel as if I am playing chess with the grim reaper in *The Seventh Seal*, my only reassurance being that Max von Sydow, who played the young knight with hair so blond it lights a fire on the screen, is now very old and maybe such fate is in store for me also.

The tuning in or rather, the pushing of buttons on the television remote is producing, at least for me, some anguish as I am spotting a trend among the commercials that appear during not only the news programs but also Jeopardy and even shows I can't recall.

No, this lack of recall has nothing to do with age; it has to do with reading in front of the television and looking up, drawn to the commercials like a moth to a flame. But my memory of the commercials is irritatingly flame-retardant.

Before I discuss the commercials, I want to make it clear that my wife and I get our news and other information also from the Internet, so we are not the "stereotypical" older person, whatever that stereotype is, in anyone's mind, including ours.

Having gotten this protestation out of the way, it is time to recall and comment what troubles me so about the commercials. In one sentence, the commercials can be summarized as being about products that either make something go up or down better. Add to that items that will make the whole process of going up or down smoother.

Let me illustrate. How many commercials do I have to watch featuring a man who can hitch his horse trailer or keep his engine from overheating before heading to a tent that is lit and a house waiting with the light on. It is as if having been transported into a strange scene of *The Great Gatsby* with that light at the end of dock.

If that is not enough, be sure to get ready to take separate baths in a commercial where the men have gray hair and the women most often don't. And why is it that the woman must look so happy that the man is taking an interest in her crossword puzzle or appetizers all of a sudden? That man must be hard up to feign interest in her filling in blank squares, and both of them must lack imagination to wear football jerseys that simply read "football team" with numbers revealing nothing alluring.

Before the 50+ crowd eats these appetizers it must be reminded by none other than Larry the Cable Guy that what goes down must come up, unless the medication that sounds so ugly in drawn-out, redneck pronunciation has been taken. Does turning 50 mean I am susceptible to pitches by Larry the Cable Guy? Let's bring to life, on the other end of the spectrum, William F. Buckley, the way they have done commercials with other dead "greats." Or at least give us George Plimpton.

When the 50+ crowd has finished these appetizers – or any time really – they must in commercial land bounce on a trampoline and eat candy animal likenesses that will add to the word regularity, which can be interpreted in many ways, but surely only with one end in mind. Of course vitamins for us 50+ folks should keep us hiking with the kind of vigor that will leave the Energizer Bunny panting somewhere on a forest path.

Finding it hard to breathe at 50+? Well, suck in this and you can get up and go exercise with your dog and gain your wife's approval, or if you are motivated more by fear, if you inhale, you will not miss out on taking your grandchildren fishing. You will not rest before your time in your casket, and bless you too, Mr. Orson Welles. Remember him and those wine commercials? Yes, you are old enough and your mind works a lot better than you think it does.

All this activity, ranging from G to XXX makes one sweaty and in need of presentable cleanliness. Why, there he is, that famous singer I used to watch with his daughter advertising a skin cream. He is singing a different tune now, and it's all about getting yourself into the bath without having to step over the sides of a tub. If they only played Bobby Darin's "Splish Splash," I would like this demonstration more.

Wow! They must have made a mistake because surely this is not for us "old" people. There is beef all of a sudden. A hot young woman eating in a way that reminds me I should buy blood pressure medication has come on. And, a guy is appearing on the beach also. Beef for everyone! Now there is a commercial finally for those of us who are 50+! ☕

A Brief History of the American Family Vacation

Back in the good old days, certainly in the 1970s and earlier, when many American families took their annual vacations together, it meant four people packing themselves and their suitcases – dusted off once a year for the occasion – into an automobile. Dad did most of the driving during this one week set aside from toiling and working on the American Dream to give the family a vacation proper; in some modern families Mom relieved Dad of some driving duties just enough to allow him to preserve his manhood. In the back seat, like caged animals best separated, sat the offspring in various constellations of brother and sister.

You can see them now, can't you? Dad tired from driving all day, because part of the bragging rights to a vacation meant recording a massive amount of miles with minimal bathroom breaks, all on a mission to gaze upon a national park or two or three, depending on the parents' willingness to subject themselves to masochism, in the spirit of broadening the horizons of their children. Just when they could take no more, Jane and Jimmy were let out of the car as they spotted an orange roof top or a motel that had doors facing outward and to which the respectable middle-class family could drive up. Those were the days, when such motels were in fashion and did not mean crime, prostitution or rent-by-the week for the economically distressed.

A swimming pool, perhaps with curves and the obligatory diving board were the reward at the end of the day; so was a buffet where children under 12 ate for free, lots of Wrigley's Spearmint gum jawed by the kids to make up for kinesthetic inactivity during the long trek of middle-class righteousness, a bottle of hard liquor for the parents, a trip to the noisy ice machine to make it on the rocks, and photos of varying quality to be turned into slides - those were the mementos of an American, God-given family vacation.

Cut to the present, where families spend more than they can afford to take children to Disney World, Hawaii, Europe and all sorts of snow sport destinations that involve anything but skis. And lately, the selfie-stick has been added to iPhone mono-ramas of spending sprees tweeted or posted foolishly on Facebook or platforms for younger persons while the family is still in the process of "experiencing" something to brag about... mostly how they are able to spoil their children.

Besides empty wallets or, more likely, maxed out credit cards, this type of modern vacation leaves souvenirs of bad taste in the mouth of anyone with even reasonably sound fiscal responsibility and mind, and resentment toward the children who have been busy on social media while not even looking away from their smartphone to see the Grand Canyon.

The vacations of Americans clearly need an overhaul. With this renaissance will also come fiscal responsibility and saving. Children are spoiled year round with all sorts of enrichment activities that cost money, often in the name of preparing to get into a good college, even while still in preschool. What follows are some suggestions for a meaningful vacation experience. Just about anyone who is not a toddler can participate (and what use is it anyway to bring along a toddler traveling across America or Europe).

1. This summer have your child chop wood. That's right, wood. Purchase logs you can narrowly fit into your gulp-sized carbon footprint SUV or on its rack, then give your youngster an axe. A 10-year-old should be able to split wood in preparation for consumption during a long, hard winter. As I recall, when I was seven years old, my father gave me a beautiful knife and I was soon biking with it, in its sheath, stopping only to shell the bark of anything remotely resembling a tree.

2. If you want your child to learn knife skills, have him or her peel potatoes every night for a meal that includes potato salad – food children who are now grown and contributing members of society used to eat. If you are going to spoil your children this summer by letting them eat french fries, that luxury could offer

an opportunity for them to learn to clean the kitchen and leave everything spotless.

3. While on the subject of leaving everything spotless, developing dexterity – while still having the advantage of possessing flexible bones – will give your child the summer vacation experience of cleaning baseboards in your home. Summers are long, so the opportunity should legitimately arise with frequency, avoiding any accusations that you are providing simulated activities such as the commercial dreck to be had at Disney World.

4. We have of course not yet touched on mowing the lawn, that all-American ritual of ownership and stewardship with sweat on more than the brow, but walking behind a push mower should be a no-brainer for a fun vacation activity. Doing the laundry is another one. Cleaning toilets, really cleaning toilets, not the way commercial services do it. I am certain you can come up with a list for a chore-vacation that your child and you will remember for years to come.

We spoil our children year round, and this year, before you plan any expensive diversions, keep things close to home by setting up a chore-vacation the whole family can enjoy, the whole summer, until school tolls. There is something to be said for family togetherness during vacations. Can't you visualize yourself sitting in the kitchen having a drink while your children are rubbing and wiping the baseboards, or you're sipping a glass of wine as the day cools and your child mows the lawn, or you affectionately look on while enjoying a beer and teaching your child the life skill of peeling potatoes on a kitchen island.

What to do with the money saved this summer? If you are a kind and caring parent, you can put the money into your child's college savings account. If you are more like the government, take the money and treat your significant other and yourself to a weekend away from the family vacation. You deserve it, because you have helped establish the birth of a new kind of vacation: chores for your children. America will truly be a better country for it. ❦

The Great American Lawn Mowing

When I was growing up, during formative years that seemed very long and agonizing, my father tried to teach my brother and me "the value of a dollar." A major, memorable way in which he practiced this slow step toward illustrating the American Dream, as if we were puppets of this demonstration, was to have us mow the lawn.

I am here not concerned with my brother's experience, because somehow due to maternal intervention it was quickly determined he had allergies and was thus exempt from walking back and forth, back and forth behind a lawnmower in 100 plus degree Texas heat – which meant that as a teenager fit from repeated bouts of this hard labor I was soon able to finish mowing the lawn in two and a half hours.

At the time I did not understand the value of earning a dollar, on which my father appeared so fixated, nor why I had to suffer at the work-ethic hands of a father who apparently thought I would never know what it was like to grow up as a child in post-World War II Germany; somehow he connected my twice a week lawn mowing sessions with his tough past, while ceding to my Swedish mother. In Dallas, a well-fertilized and sprinkled lawn required uber-frequent mowings, which would have suited my father just fine – he did not want his eldest son to turn out to be one of those kids going to a "fancy-pants" school where my only sweat might come from yielding a lacrosse stick and pain in my ankle from twisting it on a tennis court. Instead, dazed from the heat and extended sessions of labor, I had to walk into metal sprinkler heads and stumble, and if I was not paying attention and nicked them, I was made well aware, even back then, that one head cost $25 and other injurious parts were included in the experience. The value of a dollar must be multiplied many times to reach the full amount of $25.

As I walked behind the self-propelled mower - which my father proudly proclaimed was "self-propelled" to anyone who would listen, as if this feature was an incredible luxury and feat of technology - I did not understand why the neighbors truly practiced trickle-down economics and had adults come to take care of lawns so their children could lounge inside air conditioning or on the hot deck of a pool, while fathers worked in their home "studies," with framed photographs of Ronald Reagan winking at them. And my trickle-down was all across my bare back, itching from the inevitable interaction with the grass that had to be emptied into black trash bags that would burst from the heat as they were packed perfectly close to the lawn without touching it and leaving the driveway clear for a fancy automobile the American Dream was rolling along.

Yes, whether or not teenagers are conscripted to do the labor of lawn mowing, they will bite the hand that feeds them. The question now (after many years of enjoying mowing my own lawn, before beginning to practice trickle-down economics and having it treated like a mistress: styled, blown and fertilized to consummate perfection with a jewel-worthy huge carbon footprint to top the trophy possession), is if my laborious encounter with the lawn and lessons of the value of a dollar make me a better American and contributor to society? Did being called out from my room where I was reading benefit anyone other than my father and his notions of what it takes to raise a son who would make him as proud as the American flag and Republican party?

I think of Walt Whitman now, and his obsession with grass, and his famous lines from, what else, *Leaves of Grass* - a state of mind I am certain my father did not intend - and it is too easy to pluck "Resist much, obey little" or my favorite, "If you want me again look for me under your boot soles" as a reminder that a) I fought mowing for money all the way, and b) my father is now dead and cannot see how I turned out as an adult walking through life, often on carpet or flooring. Should we put "fancy-pants" Trevor out there in the heat with a lawnmower and let him have his long walks to mull things over this growing season of 2015? Will it make a difference? If so, what kind of difference. It doesn't matter, just put him out there. Unless, of course, he has asthma and you are not willing to pay for the pharmaceutical treatments, more expensive than the trickle-down lawn care, just to prove what point. ✒

Summer School in the Garden

This morning I caught the beginning of the end of the white petals raining on the lawn, the crepe myrtle trees that have brought shade and such beauty, peace as I have stolen moments outside on the back porch. I viewed them like an outsider, as if I did not belong there, as I raised my iPhone to photograph them, as if I could capture exact beauty.

This is how I have taken breaks teaching American literature online this A-term: getting up to stretch and venturing into our backyard, a garden more beautiful than I am deserving as a mere mortal navigating whether Emily killed Homer Barron in "A Rose for Emily" or if Theodore Roethke really identified with "Cuttings" or pulling weeds.

Those are of course examples that have to do with nature, including human nature. But most of the works we've read have been dark, devoid of nature's beauty to soften the blows of characters not achieving the American Dream in Sherwood Anderson's tales, in which people practically bury themselves alive, or in Toni Morrison's "Recitatif" where they get swept up in disliking "the other side."

I have discovered this summer what a hibiscus looks like. I have seen the developmental phases of agapanthus, and as I have come to know them all (with apologies to paraphrasing from "The Love Song of J. Alfred Prufrock" just now), I have taken photographs with ease using my iPhone. Oh the butterflies I can show you from my leaning into the buddleia, also known as butterfly bush. I do not know the name of the winged crusader, but if you look at the beautiful blue part of his black wings, I am sure you can identify him.

Bumble bees have been my companions when bleary-eyed from the computer screen on which I have just read that Harry, in Hemingway's "Snows of Kilimanjaro," is not nice to his wife and that the hyena in the story is symbolic of death. The green humming bird I have seen has been a welcome antidote to an electronic stack of students dutifully chronicling abysmal behavior of characters inhabiting a thick anthology.

Watering has been one of my favorite breaks, moving a sprinkler attached to the garden hose, an excuse to explore other corners of our backyard I do not see during the regular academic year. Asked by my wife to please water the hydrangea, I managed to identify that they were the beautiful light-blue blooms that to me look very much like the flowers of crepe myrtles, off the fence near our neighbor to the right side of the house. No, I did not have any thoughts about "good fences make good neighbors" when I went to turn on the water.

That has been part of the beauty of teaching English online this summer with the garden just outside. It clears and cleans the mind and head quickly, so that when I go inside I am new to the students' work. What a difference from walking down the grey carpet against institutional cream-colored walls to explore the alphabetic choices of the snack machine and see if the wish pushed for is a match. Here, in my wife's garden proper, I see the cherry tomatoes, peppers, smell mint, even recognize by sight that the small orange flowers planted next to this garden are a natural way to keep pests from attacking what grows on the vine.

I return inside, try to remember to sit up straight, place my fingers on the keyboard, neck straight, and continue to type the thoughts of summer school. ❦

If you liked this book you may want to stay informed of other things going on in the Swedish and Swedish American community in America – the easiest way is with a subscription to Nordstjernan – America's oldest, yet contemporary periodical, a tradition since 1872. A subscription will pay for itself through the special offers you are eligible for. See a sample of content and continuously updated news from Swedish America at *www.nordstjernan.com*.

You will find all of the books we publish or print at *www.NordicSampler.com*, a website we share with our sister publication *Nordic Reach*.

www.ingramcontent.com/pod-product-compliance
Lightning Source LLC
Chambersburg PA
CBHW060120260626
47160CB00005B/1946